CHICAGO PUBLIC

W9-BYU-938

R02007 60343

"Would you want me if I wasn't a virgin?"

Had he been standing, the question would have knocked him over. There were a thousand safe ways to answer that question. A thousand games he could play with her. Instead Kevin stared into Haley's eyes and knew he could only tell her the truth.

"I want you now. The difference is if you weren't a virgin, I'd act on it."

He'd hoped that would send her running, but Haley, being Haley, crossed to the bed and sat next to him. Before he could gather his defenses, she leaned forward and kissed him....

NORTH AUSTIN BRANCH
5724 W. NORTH AVE.
CHICAGO, IL 60639

Dear Reader,

Love is in the air, but the days will certainly be sweeter if you snuggle up with this month's Special Edition offerings— and a box of decadent chocolates. First up, award-winning author and this year's President of Romance Writers of America®, Shirley Hailstock is a fresh new voice for Special Edition, but fans already know what a gifted storyteller she is. With numerous novels and novellas under her belt, Shirley debuts in Special Edition with *A Father's Fortune*, which tells the story of a day-care-center owner and her foster child who teach a grumpy carpenter how to face his past and open his heart to love.

Lindsay McKenna packs a punch in *Her Healing Touch,* a fast-paced read from beginning to end. The next in her widely acclaimed MORGAN'S MERCENARIES: DESTINY'S WOMEN series, this romance details the trials of a beautiful paramedic who teaches a handsome Special Forces officer the ways of her legendary healing. *USA TODAY* bestselling author Susan Mallery *completely* wins us over in *Completely Smitten*, next up in her beloved series HOMETOWN HEARTBREAKERS. Here, an adventurous preacher's daughter seeks out a new life, but never expects to find a new *love* with a sexy U.S. marshal.

The fourth installment in Crystal Green's KANE'S CROSSING miniseries, *There Goes the Bride* oozes excitement when a runaway bride is spirited out of town by a reclusive pilot she once loved in high school. Patricia McLinn delights her readers with *Wedding of the Century*. Here, a heroine returns to her hometown seven years after running out of her wedding. When she faces her jilted groom, she realizes their feelings are stronger than ever! Finally, in Leigh Greenwood's *Family Merger*, sparks fly when a workaholic businessman meets a good-hearted social worker, who teaches him the meaning of love.

Don't miss this array of novels that deliver an emotional charge and satisfying finish you're sure to savor, no matter what the season!

Happy Valentine's Day!

Karen Taylor Richman
Senior Editor

Please address questions and book requests to:
Silhouette Reader Service
U.S.: 3010 Walden Ave., P.O. Box 1325, Buffalo, NY 14269
Canadian: P.O. Box 609, Fort Erie, Ont. L2A 5X3

Susan Mallery

COMPLETELY
SMITTEN

NORTH AUSTIN BRANCH
5724 W. NORTH AVE.
CHICAGO, IL 60639

♥ Silhouette®

SPECIAL EDITION™

Published by Silhouette Books

America's Publisher of Contemporary Romance

If you purchased this book without a cover you should be aware
that this book is stolen property. It was reported as "unsold and
destroyed" to the publisher, and neither the author nor the
publisher has received any payment for this "stripped book."

To my readers, with thanks.
And to my editor, Karen Taylor Richman.
May there be at least fifty more.

 SILHOUETTE BOOKS

ISBN 0-373-24520-3

COMPLETELY SMITTEN

Copyright © 2003 by Susan Macias Redmond

All rights reserved. Except for use in any review, the reproduction
or utilization of this work in whole or in part in any form by any
electronic, mechanical or other means, now known or hereafter
invented, including xerography, photocopying and recording, or in
any information storage or retrieval system, is forbidden without
the written permission of the editorial office, Silhouette Books,
300 East 42nd Street, New York, NY 10017 U.S.A.

All characters in this book have no existence outside the imagination of
the author and have no relation whatsoever to anyone bearing the same
name or names. They are not even distantly inspired by any individual
known or unknown to the author, and all incidents are pure invention.

This edition published by arrangement with Harlequin Books S.A.

® and TM are trademarks of Harlequin Books S.A., used under license.
Trademarks indicated with ® are registered in the United States Patent
and Trademark Office, the Canadian Trade Marks Office and in other
countries.

Visit Silhouette at www.eHarlequin.com

Printed in U.S.A.

Books by Susan Mallery

SUSAN MALLERY

is the bestselling author of over fifty books for Harlequin and Silhouette Books. She makes her home in the Pacific Northwest with her handsome prince of a husband and her two adorable-but-not-bright cats.

Dear Reader,

Completely Smitten is a milestone book for me. I have now published fifty books with Silhouette.

When I was first trying to get published, I remember thinking how much I wanted to sell just one book. The idea of actually selling two, or even ten, was unimaginable. Yet being a writer was my dream and nothing was going to defeat me.

I would love to tell you that I sold the first book I wrote, but no. I sent in many projects before Silhouette bought one. It took me a year to sell my second book to them. Slowly, I learned what they expected of me and what I could expect of them.

Writing is very personal. There are bits and pieces of my life in many of my stories and parts of myself in every heroine. Friends tell me they can "hear my voice" in some of the dialogue. My writing expresses my world view—that we are all made better by the act of loving, that family matters, that we all need to try to be the best person we can be.

I write because it is what I love to do. It is more than my career—it is my passion. I am grateful for the opportunity to write for Silhouette Books and I thank you, my readers, for your continued support.

Here's to the next fifty books!

Susan Mallery

R0200760343

Chapter One

All Kevin Harmon wanted was a beer, a burger and a bed, in that order. He'd had the kind of day designed to make a man rethink his career choices. He'd been bit, he was stuck in the middle of Kansas on a night that was practically guaranteed to produce twisters, and he'd just been offered a promotion. Not one thing was going right with his life. For once he wasn't looking for trouble, so of course trouble came looking for him.

He'd been around long enough to know that when a pretty, wide-eyed blonde walked into a seedy roadside bar, somewhere, somehow, there was going to be hell to pay. Kevin was determined to stay out of the way. No matter what.

He turned his attention from the petite blonde back

to the bartender. "Burger," he said, pushing the plastic menu back at the man. "Extra fries."

The bartender nodded and wrote something on a pad of paper, then set a frosty mug down on a once-white coaster advertising the local grange.

Kevin took a long drink. He'd just spent the better part of the day transporting a convicted felon across state lines. The process had not gone smoothly, which explained the bite on his arm. The skin hadn't been broken, but he really hated when there was trouble on the road. If he hadn't drawn the short straw, he would be down in Florida, helping with a drug raid. But no, he was stuck in Kansas where the air was so thick you could practically stand a spoon up in midair. The pressure was rising—or maybe falling—he could never remember which one caused storms to spin out of control and become tornados.

He'd grown up with twisters, back when he'd lived in Texas, and he'd never liked them. They always seemed to show up right when he was supposed to be whipping the crosstown rival at a baseball game.

Kevin thought about tornados and Texas. He even tried to remember if he needed to buy milk when he flew home the next day. Anything to keep from turning to watch the progress of the blonde. It wasn't that she was so attractive that he couldn't resist her. Far from it. Sure, she was pretty enough, but pretty was a dime a dozen.

Instead, what made him determined to stay out of it was the nervousness he'd seen lurking in her eyes, and the hesitation in her step. She belonged in this bar as much as a dog with mange belonged in church.

The bartender flipped on a small television. Instantly the sound of a ball game blasted into the half-full room. Kevin continued to drink his beer, while he stared determinedly at the screen. He ignored everything else, even the half sly, half defiant male laughter behind him.

Bullies moving in for the kill.

He swore under his breath as he set his mug on the bar and pulled off his cap. The one with U.S. Marshals embroidered on the front. He was hot, he was tired, he was hungry. The last thing he wanted tonight was a fight.

Since when did fate pay any attention to what he wanted?

He turned on the bar stool and surveyed the situation. The blonde stood between two big guys with more tattoos than sense. A third, smaller man, had his hand on her arm.

She was of medium height, maybe five-four or five-five, with short hair and big eyes, more blue than hazel. There wasn't a speck of makeup on her face, but she was still attractive, with full lips and a stubborn-looking chin.

Her clothing choices made him wince. The shapeless short-sleeved dress she wore fell nearly to her ankles. It looked ugly enough to be embarrassed to be a dust cloth—with a white lace collar and some god-awful flower print. What was it about women and clothes with plants on them?

Kevin approached the quartet. The blonde struggled to break free of the little guy's hold. When she looked up and saw him, relief filled her eyes.

"You with them?" he asked, getting more tired by the second.

She shook her head.

Kevin turned his full attention on the man holding her arm. "Then, son, you'd best let the lady go."

One of the big guys took a step toward him. Kevin flexed his hands.

"I've had a bad day, gentlemen. I'm hungry, tired, and not in the mood. So you can walk away right now, or we can move it outside. I feel obliged to warn you that if we take this to the next level, the only one walking away will be me."

Haley couldn't believe it. She felt as if she was in one of those Clint Eastwood Dirty Harry movies her dad liked so much. She half expected to see the dark-haired man pull out a .357 Magnum and ask someone to make his day.

Instead, the skinny man with rabbit teeth who'd been holding her arm let go. He took a step back, holding up his hands and trying to smile.

"We didn't mean nothin'. Just thought the lady would like some company."

His two friends nodded. They were big. Bigger than her rescuer. A couple of their tattoos had interesting swearwords woven into the designs. She'd been trying to read them when Mr. Rabbit Teeth had grabbed her.

The three of them threw some bills on their table and left. Haley breathed a sigh of relief.

"That was something," she said earnestly. "I didn't know what to do. I mean, when he wouldn't let go. I thought about screaming, but it's kind of embarrassing to have to do that. I didn't want to make a fuss.''

The man who had come to her assistance didn't say anything. Instead, he headed back toward the bar and slid onto his stool. She followed.

"Thank you for rescuing me," she said.

"Make a fuss," he said, reaching for his beer.

She sat next to him. "What?"

He took a long swallow, then stared at her over the mug. "Next time you get in trouble, make a fuss. Better yet, next time stay out of bars."

Haley reached out to tug on a strand of her hair, only to remember too late that she'd cut it all off the previous afternoon. Instead of a long braid nearly to her waist, she had short bits of fluff flying around her head.

She smoothed what was left of her bangs, then nodded. Stay out of bars. It was probably good advice. "I just can't," she said with a sigh. "Not yet."

The man stared at her. "You have a death wish?"

She laughed. "I'm not going to get killed. I just need to handle things better." She scooted a little closer and lowered her voice. "Do you know that until two days ago I'd never been in a bar before?"

Her rescuer stared at her in disbelief.

"I know," she said. "I've led a very sheltered life. It's pathetic. I mean, I'm twenty-five years old and I've been living like a nun." She shrugged. "Not that I'm Catholic. We're Baptists. My dad's a minister at our church."

The man didn't say anything. He turned his attention to the baseball game on the television. Haley studied his strong profile. He was handsome, in a rugged, cigarette-advertisement sort of way. There was an air of strength about him. He looked people in the eye when he spoke and she liked that. He wore his dark hair short.

She reached over and picked up his U.S. Marshals cap, then ran her fingers along the stitching. "So you're like a cop?"

"Sort of."

"I'll bet you're a good one."

He turned his attention back to her. She noticed he had brown eyes the color of chocolate, and while he'd yet to smile at her, she liked the shape of his mouth.

"How the hell would you know that?" he asked, sounding gruff and annoyed.

His tone made her spine stiffen just a little, while the swearword startled her. He's said the H-word. Just like that. She would bet that he hadn't even planned it. The word had just come out.

One day she was going to swear, too. She would casually drop the H-word or the D-word into conversation. But that was all. Swearing was one thing, but really bad words were just ugly.

He waved a hand in front of her face. "Are you still in there?"

"Oh. Sorry. What was the question?"

"Never mind."

She put his hat back on the bar. "I'm Haley Foster." She held out her hand.

He stared at it for a long time before taking it in his and shaking. "Kevin Harmon."

"Nice to meet you, Kevin."

He grunted and turned back to the television.

Haley shifted slightly on her stool and took in the ambience of the location. There were several posters of various sports, some advertisements for alcoholic beverages. The floor was dirty, and some of the tables looked as if they hadn't been wiped off in a while. Except for a woman with an incredibly large bosom in the corner, she seemed to be the only female in the place.

She glanced at her watch. It was nearly eight. "Why aren't there more women here?" she asked.

Kevin never took his gaze off the game. "It's not that kind of place."

"What kind of place?"

"This isn't the kind of bar where you bring a date."

There were different kinds of bars? "How do you know that?"

"I just know."

A not very helpful answer.

The bartender walked over. "What can I get you?"

Haley eyed Kevin's beer. Yesterday she'd had her first glass of white wine ever. To be honest, she hadn't really liked it.

"A margarita," she said.

"Frozen or on the rocks?"

The only liquor question she knew the answer to was James Bond's, "Shaken, not stirred." Okay, rocks were ice. On the rocks would mean over ice, which wasn't how she pictured margaritas.

"Frozen," she said. "Oh. Do you have any of those little umbrellas to put in the glass?"

The bartender stared at her. "No."

"Too bad." She'd always wanted a drink with a little umbrella.

She watched as the man poured various liquids into a blender. He added a scoop of ice, then set the whole thing to whirling and crunching. When he finally put a glass in front of her, the light green concoction looked more like a slushy drink than anything else.

"Thanks."

She took a sip from the tiny straw the bartender had dropped into her glass.

The first thing she noticed was the cold. The second was the flavor. Not sweet, but not bitter, either. Kind of lime, kind of something else.

"It's good," she said in surprise. It was sure better than that wine she'd had the previous night. She turned her attention back to Kevin.

"So why are you here?"

He turned slowly until his dark gaze rested on her face. He was really very handsome. She found herself wishing she hadn't been quite so quick to cut off all her hair. Allan had always said it was her best feature.

Allan. She took a long drink of her margarita. She did *not* want to think about him. Not now. Not ever.

"Are you asking my spiritual purpose in the universe?" Kevin asked.

"Only if you want to tell me. I was thinking more of, do you live around here? What are you doing in the bar? That sort of thing."

He finished his beer and pushed the glass across the bar. "Another," he called before turning his attention back to her. "What are *you* doing here? In this bar. Today."

"Well…" She took another long sip. "I'm driving to Hawaii."

Kevin wished he'd changed the order of his wants back when life had still been sane. If he'd wanted a *bed,* a beer and a burger, he would now be in some hotel, ordering room service and watching the game in peace. Instead, he was having a conversation with a woman who had left the functioning part of her brain back in her car.

"Hawaii?"

Haley beamed at him. "Okay, so I know you can't *really* drive to Hawaii, but I'm going to get as close as possible."

"That would be California."

"Right. I'll figure out the rest of it when I get there."

"Where are you driving from?"

"Western Ohio. I'm—"

But whatever she'd been about to confess was cut off by the arrival of his dinner. Haley stared at the large plate containing a burger on a bun—the top of the bun covered with lettuce, tomatoes and onion— along with a mound of fries that threatened to fall onto the counter.

"You can get food in a bar?" she asked, incredulous. "For real?"

He remembered walking to school years ago and seeing a starving dog. The dirty brown-and-white fur ball had been hiding in an alley. Kevin had taken one look at its shivering, skinny self, then he'd handed over his sandwich. He'd gone without lunch for two days before finally taking the dog home.

"You're broke," he said flatly, wondering when his luck had gotten so bad. He pushed the plate toward her. "Eat up."

She took another drink of her margarita. "Broke?" She swallowed. "No. I have money."

She put the glass on the bar, then pulled a small purse that had been dangling off one shoulder onto her lap and opened it. Inside was a wad of bills.

"I cleaned out my savings account," she said, then lowered her voice. "I have the rest of it in traveler's checks. It's really much safer that way." The purse closed with a snap.

She took another drink, then gasped and slapped her hands over her face.

"Ouch. Oh, yuck. It hurts. It hurts." She shimmied on the bar stool, alternately cupping her nose and mouth and waving her hand back and forth.

Kevin pulled his plate in front of him, then nodded at the bartender. "Could we have a glass of water?"

The bartender filled a glass and passed it over to Haley. She gulped some down. After a couple of swallows, she sighed.

"Much better." She put the glass down. "I had one of those flash ice headaches."

"We all knew that."

She half stood, stretched over the bar and snagged a small plate. "Want to share your fries?"

"Why not?"

She scooped several onto her plate and crunched the first one.

He was in hell, he decided, watching her. Somewhere in his day, he'd died and this was God's way of punishing him for all the screwing up he'd done in his life.

"So I'm from Ohio," she said with a smile. "Western Ohio. A little town you've never heard of. Have you been to Ohio?"

"Columbus."

"It's nice, huh?"

"A wonderful place."

She nodded, not coming close to catching the sarcasm in his voice.

Why him? That's what he wanted to know. There were probably twenty other guys in the bar. Why had he been the one to come to her rescue? Why hadn't someone else stepped in?

"Like I said, my dad's a minister." She ate another French fry, then drank more of her margarita. "My mom died when I was born, so I don't remember her. The thing is, when you're the preacher's kid, everybody feels responsible for keeping you on the straight and narrow. I didn't have one mother—I had fifty. I couldn't even think something bad before it was being reported to my dad."

"Uh-huh."

Kevin turned back to the game and tried not to listen.

"So that's why I don't know the bar thing."

"What bar thing?" he asked before he could stop himself.

"That this isn't a bar people bring their dates to. I'm practicing being bad."

That got his attention. He swung back to face her. "Bad?"

"You bet." She finished her margarita and pushed her glass to the edge of the counter. "I'd like another one, please," she said, then beamed at the bartender. "It was great."

She turned back to Kevin. "I just wish I could have a little umbrella."

He didn't care about that. "Tell me about being bad."

"I haven't been. Ever. So that's what I'm doing on my drive to Hawaii." She glanced around as if to make sure no one was listening. "This is only my third time in a bar."

"You're kidding," he said, more because he was hoping she wasn't telling the truth than because he didn't believe her.

"When I left home three days ago, I'd never even had anything alcoholic to drink. So that first night, when I stopped, I went into a bar." She bit into another fry and wrinkled her nose. Humor crinkled the corners of her eyes.

"It was horrible," she said when she'd swallowed. "I felt so out of place and when a man smiled at me, I ran out the door. Yesterday was better."

He gave up. There was no point in avoiding what was obviously his fate. "Your second time in a bar?"

She nodded. "I had white wine, but I have to tell you I didn't like it at all. But I did almost speak to someone."

Great.

The bartender finished blending the margarita and set it in front of her. "Want to run a tab?" he asked.

Haley pressed her lips together for a couple of seconds. "Maybe," she said at last.

"Yes," Kevin said. "Run her a tab. You want your own order of fries?"

"Okay. Extra salt, please."

The bartender muttered something under his breath, then wrote on his small pad.

"A tab," Kevin said when they were alone, "means they keep a list of what you've ordered. You pay once at the end of the evening instead of paying each time."

Haley's blue-hazel eyes widened. "That's so cool."

He had a feeling the world was going to be one constant amazement after the other for her.

He studied her pale skin, her wide smile and trusting eyes. This was not a woman who should be let out on her own.

"You need to think about heading back to Ohio."

"No way." She took a long drink of her margarita. "I've spent my entire life doing what everyone else has told me to do. Now I'm only doing what I want. No matter what."

Her expression turned fierce. "You can't know what it's like," she continued. "I never get to voice my opinion. If I even try, I get ignored. No one cares what I think or what I want."

"That's why you're running away?"

"Exactly." She picked up a French fry, then put it

back on the plate. "How did you know I was running away?"

"You're not the kind of woman to come to a place like this on purpose."

She glanced around at the seedy clientele, then shrugged. "I want new experiences."

"Like little umbrellas in your drinks?"

"Exactly."

She smiled. He had to admit she had a great smile. Her whole face lit up. He would have guessed her age to be mid-twenties, but in some ways she acted more like an awkward teenager than a grown woman. No doubt being the daughter of a single father minister had something to do with it.

He thought about suggesting that next time she find her new experience at a more upscale bar, but then he reminded himself he wasn't getting involved. He had enough problems of his own without adding her to the list.

"It's not that I don't like the *piano*," she said.

"What?"

"The piano. I play. It was expected. I can also play the organ, but only a few hymns and not very well."

"Okay." He started eating his burger.

"The music is great. But I wanted to be a teacher."

"Your father objected?" he asked before he could stop himself.

She sighed. "He would never come out and tell me no. That's not his way. But there was subtle pressure. In a way that's a whole lot harder to resist. I mean, a direct statement can be argued, but hints and nudges kind of sweep you along until you suddenly wake up and find yourself in a place you don't want to be."

She took another long drink of her margarita. The

bartender appeared with a plate of fries. Haley smiled her thanks.

Kevin finished his burger and thought about making his escape.

"You want me to replace what I took?" she asked, motioning to his plate.

"No thanks."

She shrugged, then munched on another fry. "So you're a U.S. Marshal. What do you?"

"I just delivered a prisoner to the federal penitentiary up the road."

Her eyes widened. "There's a prison here?"

"Didn't you see the signs about not picking up hitchhikers?"

"Sure, but I thought it was some kind of joke. You know, a local gag on tourists."

"This isn't a real tourist haven. Most of the folks are passing through or here to visit relatives."

She glanced over her shoulder, then leaned close and lowered her voice. "People here know men in prison?"

He groaned. "Haley, have you ever been outside of your hometown before?"

"Of course. I spent four years at the Southern Baptist College for Young Women."

Just perfect. "And after your college experience?"

"I went back home, where I got my master's in music and finished up the courses I needed for my teaching credentials. I graduated with honors."

She reached for her glass. Her hand missed the stem by about three inches. She stretched out her fingers, then curled them into her palm.

"My skin feels funny," she said. "My cheeks tingle."

Kevin swore silently. He glanced at the nearly finished second drink, then turned his attention to the bartender drying glasses with a dirty towel.

"Doubles?" he asked.

The old man grinned. "Thought you might want to get lucky."

Perfect. Just perfect. In less than forty minutes the nondrinking preacher's daughter had just consumed the equivalent of four shots of tequila. The full effect of the alcohol wasn't going to hit for about twenty more minutes. He would bet a week's salary that she would be on her butt about thirty seconds after that.

He slapped some money onto the bar and stood. "Come on, Haley. I'm going to get you out of here while you can still walk. Have you got a hotel room?"

She blinked at him. "I can walk."

"Sure you can. Why don't you try?"

She wore the ugliest beige shoes he'd ever seen, but at least the heel wasn't too high. When she slid off the stool, she stood straight just long enough to give him hope. Maybe he'd overreacted. Maybe—

She swayed so far to the left, she nearly toppled over.

"Am I drunk?" she asked, sounding delighted as she managed to stand straight. "The room is spinning. Wow. This is so cool."

Yeah, everything was cool to her. "Do you have a motel room?" he repeated, speaking slowly and deliberately.

"Yeah. The pink one. I liked the color. It's over there. Outside."

She pointed to the exit and nearly fell on her face. Kevin gritted his teeth.

"Put your arm around my shoulders," he instructed as he wrapped an arm around her waist.

His first impression was of heat; his second, of slender curves that got his body's attention in a big way.

Instead of following orders, Haley simply sagged against him. "You smell good," she said as he half carried her toward the door.

"Thanks."

He would get her to her motel and leave, he told himself. She would probably pass out in a matter of seconds and wake up with a hangover big enough to cure her of ever wanting another margarita. She'd made it this far without him, she would get to wherever she was going without his assistance.

Kevin knew he was trying to convince himself that he wasn't responsible for Haley. Unfortunately he wasn't doing a very good job.

They stepped into the sultry evening air. Haley sucked in a deep breath, then turned to look at him. As she was leaning against him, her face rested on his shoulder. Her mouth was inches from his. One of her wisps of blond hair brushed against his cheek.

"So," Haley said, licking her lips. "Is this where you take advantage of me?"

"What?"

She blinked slowly, then smiled. "I don't think I'd mind."

Chapter Two

She wouldn't mind?

Kevin did his best to ignore the sexual desire that slammed into him the second she spoke the words. His unexpected attraction to Haley couldn't begin to matter. Not with circumstances being what they were. She was drunk, alone, out of her element and, with his luck, a virgin. Thanks, but not tonight.

Lightning cut across the sky, as if warning him the Almighty was keeping tabs on the evening's events. With that in mind, Kevin ignored the curves pressing against his body and the way those curves made him feel. She might be a little slimmer than he'd first realized, but she seemed to have everything in the right place under her ugly dress. Not that he was going to be checking her out.

"Did you say a pink motel?" he asked, looking

around at the motor inns on both sides of the highway.

"Uh-huh. There's flamingos." She blinked at him. "I like birds."

"Good to know."

He spotted a low, two-story structure that matched her description. He mentally cringed at the plastic flamingos stuck into the cement. If the place looked this bad at night, what did it look like in the light of day? Of course, there was no accounting for taste.

At least they didn't have to cross the highway to get there. The motel was only a couple hundred yards up the frontage road.

"Let's start walking," he said, still supporting most of her weight.

A second bolt of lightning illuminated the sky.

"Look!" Haley said, pointing at the heavens. "Don't you love lightning? Don't you wish it would rain?"

"Sure."

Because a douse of cold water might cool him off. Drunk women begging to be taken advantage of were nothing but trouble. He had to keep reminding himself of that as Haley's soft blond hair brushed against his cheek.

He got them moving in the direction of the motel. Haley was still upright and remotely mobile, but he had a feeling that was going to be changing in the next few minutes. At least she was still managing full sentences.

"Do you know your room number?"

Rather than answer, she sighed. He felt the soft puff of air on his cheek.

"You never answered my question," she said instead.

"What question?"

He made the mistake of looking at her face—at her blue-hazel eyes and the curves at the corners of her mouth. At the knowing expression that heated his blood and made him consider possibilities.

"No way," he muttered more to himself than to her. He was *not* going there with her.

She pushed away from him and tried to stand on her own. She was nearly successful. With her feet firmly planted, she swayed back and forth, stumbled a step, then regained her balance by holding her arms out a little on each side.

"What is it about me?" she demanded. "Why don't men want to take advantage of me? Am I ugly? Is my body hideous?"

Did they really need to be having this conversation now? He eyed the night sky—thick with clouds and the promise of rain. More lightning flashed in the distance.

"We're going to get soaked in about thirty seconds," he said.

She glared at him. "I mean it. What's wrong with me?"

"Nothing's wrong with you."

"So why don't you want to have—"

For a second he thought she was actually going to say "sex" but at the last minute she pressed her lips together and stared meaningfully. At least he assumed that's what she was doing. That and tipping over.

He grabbed her around the waist and hauled her against him.

"Walk," he commanded.

She started moving.

"Tell me," she demanded. "What's wrong with me?"

"Like I said—nothing. It's not you." Hell, why not just tell her the truth? "It's the whole preacher's daughter thing. No one wants to spit in the eye of God."

She considered that while they crossed the rest of the bar's parking lot and stepped onto the motel parking lot.

"What about forbidden flute?"

The flute thing threw him for a second. "Do you mean 'fruit'?"

She nodded vigorous and nearly collapsed. "My head is spinning," she said, sounding as thrilled as a kid at a carnival. "The sky's spinning, too."

"Great."

"I can be fruit," she insisted.

"If that's what you want."

"Don't you think of me that way? Aren't I a temptation?"

He was impressed she could manage a three-syllable word. Unfortunately, while her verbal skills remained intact, her motor skills were fading fast. He had to support more and more of her weight to keep them moving toward the motel.

"Room number," he said.

"Look at what happened with Eve and the apple. That could be me. I could be an apple."

"I'll bet you could even be a plum. Keep moving."

"Plum? Who wants to be that?"

They had reached the building. Kevin paused to lean against a column supporting the overhead walkway around the second story.

"I need your key," he said. "I'm going to take it out of your purse."

She smiled brightly. "Okay."

He opened the clasp and dug around until he came up with a key attached to a plastic pink flamingo. The number three had been painted on the flamingo's wing.

At least they weren't going to have to negotiate the stairs.

She shifted her weight just as he closed her purse. The action caused her to slide against him, which pressed her right breast into his side. Instinctively he wrapped both his arms around her to hold her upright. She turned until they were facing each other. Pressed together. Close. Too close.

Her slightly unfocused eyes half closed. "You're very strong," she murmured.

"Don't even go there," he told her, trying to figure out where he was going to find room number three.

"Strong and sexy."

Before he could stop her, she reached up and pulled off his cap and stuck it on her own head. Of course she looked completely adorable.

"I've never thought about a man being strong before," she continued with a sigh. "It's nice. As for the sexy part.'' She covered her mouth with her fingers. ''I've never thought about a man that way before, either.''

''All right, Haley. Let's go.''

He got them moving toward the row of doors, each labeled with a number. There were seven on each floor.

''Do you think I'm sexy?'' she asked.

They passed seven. He didn't answer.

''Kevin?''

Six. Just three more doors and then they were home.

''Can I at least be an apple?''

Bingo. He stuck the key in the door and pushed it open.

''In we go,'' he said, helping her over the threshold.

''Not even an apple,'' she murmured, sounding tragically sad.

He told himself that speaking the truth would only get them both in trouble. In her current state there was no telling what she would do if she figured out that she was exactly like forbidden fruit and he was a man who had been starving for years.

He followed her into the room, which was typical for a cheap roadside motel. Full-size bed, small dresser, a couple of chairs and a door leading to a white-on-white bathroom. It looked clean enough, he supposed, a little surprised to find himself wanting Haley to have something nicer than this. What did he care where she stayed? As long as it wasn't with him.

He pulled the key out of the lock and closed the

door. Haley continued to hold on to him. He moved them both toward the bed so that when she finally did let go, she wouldn't have very far to fall.

Speaking of which, once he really noticed the bed—wide, covered with a blue spread and very empty—he found it hard to notice anything else.

Sexy, willing women and beds just seemed made for each other.

He had to admit he liked the feel of her pressing against him. She was warm and seemed designed to fit him. He allowed himself a brief but meaningful fantasy, then put it firmly out of his mind. For one thing, he didn't take advantage of anyone ever. For another, his track record wasn't exactly the greatest.

He dropped the key onto the small table between the chairs and put his hands on her shoulders.

"Why don't you sit down?" he suggested. "The bed is right behind you. If you're still, the room will stop spinning."

She smiled. "I like it spinning." She blinked and when she opened her eyes, her gaze lasered in on his mouth.

"Do you know that I've only ever been kissed by three men. Well, only one man, really. The other two were boys in high school." She frowned. "Or were they young men? When do boys become men?"

When they finally make it with a woman, he thought but didn't say. "Haley, you need to sit down."

Her gaze didn't waiver. "If I was fruit, you'd kiss me."

It scared him that her comment almost made sense.

"In college I didn't date much," she continued, swaying slightly so that he was forced to release her shoulders and grab her around the waist to keep her from falling. "There weren't that many boys around and the ones who were never seemed to notice me."

Then they were idiots, he thought. "Haley—"

She interrupted with a soft sigh. "I like how you say my name."

He swore silently. They were standing too close for comfort, at least for him.

"Maybe I was too good."

He stared at her, taking a second to put the statement into a logical framework. "At college?" he asked.

She nodded vigorously, then blinked several times. "I never did anything wrong."

"I'll bet."

"I don't mind doing it now." She tilted her head. "Something wrong, I mean."

"Oh, I got that." He reached up and pulled her arms from around his neck. "Sit," he said firmly.

She sat.

Her eyes widened when she hit the bed. She was eye level with his waist, which he could handle, and she seemed delighted, which he could not.

She laughed. "Okay."

Okay? Okay, what? Then he decided he didn't want to know.

Kevin pulled out one of the straight-back chairs and set it front of her. He sat and wondered if he had a prayer of reasoning with her while she was this drunk. Regardless, he had to try.

"Haley, I need you to listen to me."

"I like listening to you talk."

"Great. But pay attention to the words, too."

She sighed and nodded.

He had a bad feeling he was screaming into the wind. "You can't go around trusting people. You're drunk and vulnerable right now. That's dangerous. You can't let strange men into your motel room."

Dammit all to hell if she didn't laugh at him. "I trust you," she said.

"You shouldn't."

"Yes, I should. You're a nice man."

Nice? Perfect. Just perfect.

"Fine. I'm nice. But the next guy won't be."

"I don't want the next guy. You're my best shot at being bad."

"What?"

She shrugged and nearly toppled onto her back. He shot out a hand to steady her.

"You're nice but you're bad, too." She lowered her voice. "I can tell. I want to be bad." She leaned in close to him. "Don't you want to help me?"

What he wanted was to know what he'd done to deserve this.

She shifted on the bed, suddenly moving closer. Too close. Her gaze settled on his mouth again.

"Don't you want to kiss me?" she asked, sounding mournful. "I'd like you to, but I don't know if I'm very good at it. I've always wondered. But how do you ask? I mean, is anyone going to tell the truth? Would you tell me?"

He had no idea what they were talking about. Despite the ugly dress and her crazy, trusting personality and the fact that if he even *thought* about touching her he would be zapped by lightning, he suddenly wanted to kiss her.

He wanted to know what she would taste like and how she would respond. He wanted—

She suddenly turned from him. Her legs bumped against his as she struggled to get away. He stood, pushing the chair back, and she bolted for the bathroom. The door slammed behind her, the toilet seat went up with a clatter and two seconds later came the sounds of her being violently sick.

Kevin winced in sympathy. He was guessing this was the first time she'd been drunk, so it was probably the first time she'd been sick with alcohol. Not a fun way to end the day.

He glanced at the door, then hesitated as the need to do the right thing warred with his desire to bolt for freedom.

He compromised by deciding to stay until he knew that she was all right. At least he no longer had to worry about his virtue. There was nothing like barfing one's guts out to break the romantic mood.

Twenty minutes later it was all over but the moaning. Kevin walked to the bathroom door and knocked softly.

''Tell me you're still alive,'' he said.

A groan came in response.

He pushed the door open and found Haley curled up on the bathroom floor. Her eyes were closed, her skin the color of fog. The soft strands of blond hair now lay plastered against her forehead.

"I'm dying," she gasped.

"It only feels that way."

She shook her head, then groaned again.

"Come on," he said, crouching next to her. "Get up and take a shower. You'll feel better."

She opened one eye. "I'm never going to feel better."

"Hot water works wonders."

Her eyelids fluttered shut.

"Come on, little girl," he said, slipping his arm around her and pulling her into a sitting position.

She kept her eyes closed until she was upright, then opened them slowly.

"Is the world still spinning?" he asked.

"A little. It's not as fun as it was before."

"I'll bet." He shifted so he could unbuckle her ugly shoes. "You're probably done throwing up."

"So now I can pass away in peace?"

"Not on my watch." He pulled her up until she was sitting on the edge of the tub. "How about a change of clothes for after your shower? Do you have a robe or something?"

"I have a nightgown in the top drawer."

"Stay here. I'll go get it."

Kevin walked into the bedroom. He wasn't sure what he expected when he slid open the drawer, but any visions of lace and satin were quickly squelched when the saw the high-necked, long-sleeved, cotton granny gown.

He returned to find her sitting right where he'd left her.

"Can you stand?" he asked.

"Why would I want to?"

He chuckled.

She glared. "You should have a little more respect for the dying."

"Death is a long way off, Haley. You only wish it wasn't."

He pulled her to her feet. She swayed a little. He shifted so she had a clear line to the toilet, but she didn't bolt, so he figured they were both safe.

After pulling the plastic curtain halfway closed, he turned on the water until it was steaming hot, then adjusted the temperature to just below scalding and pulled the knob to start the spray.

He stepped back. Haley didn't budge. He gave her a little push toward the water.

"You can get in dressed or undressed," he said. "Your choice."

One hand fluttered behind her before falling back to her side. He sighed heavily, then pulled down the zipper of her dress. As he did so, he was careful not to look at anything more interesting than the sink he could see over her shoulder. He stepped back and headed for the door.

"Holler if you need anything."

"Okay."

He heard her dress hit the floor. His imagination supplied a perfect picture of everything he hadn't seen. He had a feeling the real thing would be even better.

"Kevin?"

He made the mistake of turning around before he realized the potential for disaster. Haley stood facing him, now clutching her dress to herself, but behind her was the small mirror. It reflected a slender back, narrow waist and gentle curving hips. Cream-colored perfection.

He made himself look only at her eyes. "What?"

She swallowed. "Thanks."

"No problem."

He retreated to the bedroom where he was tortured by the sounds of her in the shower. Reminding himself that she had just been sick, and probably felt less appealing than a fur ball, didn't help.

He paced restlessly for ten minutes, then forced himself to sit on the edge of the bed and click channels until he found the ball game. It was tied in the eighth inning and damned if he didn't care at all.

The shower finally went off. There were more sounds he couldn't identify, then the bathroom door opened.

Haley stood dwarfed by her cotton nightgown. The fabric hung to the floor and concealed every single curve and womanly feature. She was pale, but she no longer looked quite so desperate. Her wet hair stood up in spikes. She'd said she was twenty-five, but right now she could pass for twelve.

"I still feel pretty awful," she said.

"That'll teach you to suck down margaritas at the speed of sound. The good news is you got most of the alcohol out of your system tonight. You'll be fine in the morning."

"I hope you're right."

He stood and pulled back the covers. She slid into bed, sitting up against the pillows instead of lying down.

"You need plenty of water," he told her, filling a glass from a bottle she had on the small table. "You want to stay hydrated."

She nodded as he put the glass on the nightstand. "Are you leaving?"

Her eyes seemed bigger than before. Her mouth trembled slightly and her voice shook as she spoke. She looked like a drowned kitten.

Good sense insisted that he head out now that he knew she was all right. There was no point in staying. In the morning she could get back to whatever it was she'd been doing, and he would catch a flight back to D.C. where he was expected for a two o'clock meeting.

He stared at her, then the door. Her fingers twisted the sheet. "I'll be fine," she whispered. "You've been really nice and I don't want to take advantage of that."

He called himself eight different names, none of them fit for her ears, kicked off his shoes and sat on the bed.

"I'll stay for a little while," he said, shifting close and putting an arm around her.

She snuggled against him, resting her head on his chest where her damp hair quickly soaked his shirt. Oddly, he didn't mind.

He told himself looking after her was like caring for a child. Except she didn't feel very childlike in his arms. Nor was his reaction to her even close to paternal.

"You know all about me," she said after a few minutes. "What about you? Where are you from?"

"A place you've never heard of. Possum Landing, Texas."

She glanced up and smiled. "Possum Landing?"

He nodded. "Lived there all my life. My brother and I were born in the Dallas area."

"You have a brother?"

"Fraternal twin. Nash works for the FBI."

She sighed. "I always wanted a sister, although a brother would have been nice. Sometimes it got quiet, what with there only being me."

"Your father never remarried?"

"No. He and my mom were really in love. He used to tell me that no one could ever take her place. When I was little I thought that was really romantic, but as I got older, I thought it sounded lonely."

Kevin agreed. His mother and stepfather had a good, strong marriage, but if something happened to one of them, he would hate to think the other was destined to a solitary life. Not that he was in a position to talk. After all, he'd managed to avoid matrimonial bliss for all of his thirty-one years.

"You're a pretty young woman," he said. "How come you've only kissed three guys?"

She raised her head and looked at him. "You think I'm pretty?"

"Fishing for compliments?"

She smiled. "If you knew how seldom they came along, you wouldn't be asking the question."

He didn't like the sound of that. Why weren't people complimenting her? Then he remembered the ugly dress and even worse-looking shoes. Maybe it wasn't such a stretch to think she'd been overlooked.

"Yes, I think you're pretty," he said. "Tell me about dating."

"You mean, not dating." She dropped her head back onto his shoulder. "I can't really explain it. Some of the reason I never went out much was because I was busy with school activities and different things at church. Some of it was my dad. He used to lecture me on the importance of setting an example and doing the right thing. Plus everywhere I went in town, I knew people. They reported back any hint of unacceptable behavior."

She shifted slightly, as if getting more comfortable. The covers slipped and instead of touching layers of sheet and blanket, he suddenly found his hand resting on her hip. Only the voluminous cotton nightgown kept his fingers from touching bare skin.

He could feel the heat of her body and the arc of the curve. Ugly clothes or not, she was a woman, down to her toes. An attractive woman who, for reasons he couldn't explain, appealed to him.

Touching her hip made him think about touching other parts of her body...such as her breasts. Need flared inside, bringing his own male heat to life.

Down boy, he told himself. Not this night, not with this woman. Still, a man could dream.

"Sometimes it seemed easier not to go out," she continued, apparently unaware of the change in circumstances. "Not that there are all that many guys beating down my front door.'' She glanced up at him again. ''I'm sure you dated a lot.''

''Some.''

Color flared on her cheeks. ''You've probably even…you know.''

Uh-oh. He deliberately moved his hand away from her body and rested it on the mattress.

She cleared her throat. ''You've probably been with a woman before.''

He stared at her. ''Are you talking about sex?''

She blushed fiercely and nodded.

Hell. Why were they talking about this? ''I've had my way with a woman or two,'' he said.

''What's it like?''

Now it was his turn to groan. ''We are *not* having this conversation.''

''I know it's not appropriate, but just once I would like someone to give me some details.''

She wouldn't be getting them from him, that's for sure.

Haley sat up and looked at him. ''You've been really nice, but I'm feeling much better after the shower.'' She yawned. ''I guess I'm tired. You don't have to stay if you don't want to.''

''I know.'' He thought about leaving and realized he wasn't all that much in a hurry to go. ''I'll head out in a little while.''

She smiled at him, then. A warm, welcoming smile that stirred something in his chest. Something he hadn't felt before. Then she picked up the remote on the nightstand before settling back against him.

''Do you know they have cable here? We never

had cable. There's lots of really cool channels. Even one of those shopping shows.''

''Great,'' he muttered. ''Maybe we could finish watching the ball game instead.''

''Wouldn't you rather shop?''

''Not really.''

She laughed. ''Okay. Baseball, then shopping. How's that?''

''Sounds good.''

Kevin didn't remember falling asleep, but suddenly he came awake. Several bits of information flashed into his brain at once. First, he was in a strange bed, on top of the covers. He knew the woman in his arms, but not how she got there. Second, a man on television was holding up what looked like a pair of diamond earrings and listing all sorts of reasons one should purchase them. Third, his pager was going off.

He flipped on the lamp on the nightstand and pulled the pager from its spot on his belt. The flashing emergency code chased the last clouds of sleep from his brain. By the time Haley had stirred enough to ask what was going on, he was already on the phone.

He listened to the information, swore, then hung up.

''I have to go,'' he said as he pulled on his shoes. ''There's a riot at the prison. I need to get there now.''

Haley's blond hair had dried in spikes that stuck up all over her head. She blinked sleepily.

''A riot?''

''Yup.''

Which was exactly how his day had been going. He paused and bent long enough to scribble a number on the pad by the phone.

"This is my cell number," he said as he straightened. "Leave me a message in the morning to let me know you're okay. Agreed?"

She sat up and nodded. Her big eyes studied him. "I didn't thank you for everything."

"Thank me on the phone. I gotta run."

Kevin was out the door before Haley could think of anything else to say. She clicked off the television, then slid over to turn out the light. His side of the bed was warm. She curled up in the dark and thought about all that had happened in the past few hours. She smiled as she realized she'd finally slept with a man. All things considered, the experience had been pretty wonderful.

Chapter Three

Haley woke with the sensation that she was late. Before her eyes had focused she was trying to figure out if it was choir practice or her morning to visit the shut-ins or—

Then she blinked and realized she didn't recognize her bedroom.

In the split second it took to view the unfamiliar dresser, the window in the wrong place and the television, the events of the previous evening flashed through her mind like a silent music video. The montage included her entrance into the bar down the street, those scary men who had tried to get her to sit with them, and her rescue by Kevin Harmon. From there she recalled the margaritas, her reaction to the drinks and—

Here the memories got a little fuzzy. Or maybe it

was just that she didn't *want* to remember, because honestly, it was too embarrassing to think that she'd actually thrown herself at a man. Worse, he'd turned her down.

Haley groaned and buried her face in her pillow. The exact sequence of events wasn't clear, but she definitely recalled something about wanting to be forbidden fruit, then having to throw up. They hardly combined to make a good first impression. And through it all, Kevin had been perfect.

She sat up suddenly and brushed her too short bangs off her forehead, then stood cautiously and waited to see what her stomach was going to do. But except for an icky taste in her mouth, she felt fine. Certainly a whole lot better than she'd felt the previous night. Lying on that bathroom floor had been the closest she'd ever come to wishing for death. At least for herself.

Okay, she thought as she crossed to the bathroom, last night had been both good and bad. The good had been meeting Kevin. He'd taken care of her, treated her wonderfully, had brought her back here and stayed to make sure she was going to survive. More than that, he'd spent the night with her.

She smiled at the memory of falling asleep in his arms. Romantic things like that didn't happen to women like her.

She'd also found a drink she liked—although maybe two doubles were more than she could handle—and she'd actually spent time in a bar. If she kept this up, eventually she would be worldly.

Haley paused in front of the bathroom sink to pin

back her hair, only to remember that she'd cut it all off on her way out of Ohio. She used a headband from her small cosmetics bag to hold her bangs off her face, then turned on the water.

The bad things about last night had been getting sick and throwing herself at a man who obviously didn't find her attractive. As she splashed water on her face, she tried to figure out if she could have said or done something to make herself more appealing to Kevin. Was it something specifically about her, or was she not his type? Not that she knew what being someone's type meant. She didn't have a type that she knew of, except for "not Allan."

She straightened and pulled the hand towel from the rack. Kevin had been nice and had stayed until he'd gotten paged. So he couldn't have disliked her too much.

"There is no way you're going to figure this out," Haley told herself as she started the shower, then stripped off her nightgown. "The inner workings of the male mind are a complete mystery."

That decided, she stepped into the warm spray and contented herself with the memory of him holding her close as they stretched out together on the bed.

Thirty minutes later Haley was dressed, packed and eating a breakfast consisting of coffee made in the in-room pot and a granola bar she'd brought with her. She would have liked something more substantial, but she hadn't seen any fast-food places on her way into town and she hadn't worked up the nerve to eat alone in a regular restaurant. Plus, she wasn't sure how her stomach was going to react to a big meal just yet. Maybe it would be better to take things slow.

She sat on the bed and peeled back the wrapping on her breakfast, all the while staring at the phone number written on the small pad. Kevin's cell number. Before he'd left he'd asked her to phone to let him know she was all right. Part of her wanted to hear his voice again, but part of her was still pretty embarrassed by everything that had happened. He'd done more than enough. She shouldn't bother the poor man.

Indecision made her shift on the bed. As she nibbled on the bar, she reached for the television remote and clicked on the TV to distract herself. A well-dressed, thirty-something woman spoke directly to the camera.

"We'll go to that footage in a moment. Our live shots confirm what the authorities are telling us. The prison riot seems to have ended."

Haley stared at the screen. Prison riot? Hadn't Kevin said something about delivering a prisoner?

"As you can see from this video taken last night, several prisoners started a riot that turned violent. There were over two dozen injuries, including at least three gunshot wounds. One U.S. Marshal was taken to a local hospital at about five this morning."

As the woman spoke, the camera panned over heavily armed authorities trying to subdue angry prisoners. From there, the shot focused on a man on a stretcher. The camera zoomed in on his face. Haley dropped her granola bar and came as close to swearing as she ever had in her life. Despite the blood on his face and the thick, blood-soaked bandage around his leg, she recognized the man being rushed to the ambulance.

It was Kevin.

Okay, she was an idiot, Haley thought an hour later as she paced in the hospital waiting room. What had she been thinking when she'd decided to check on Kevin at the hospital? Or *had* she been thinking?

One second she'd been stunned by the live news report and the next she'd been loading up her car and asking the guy at the motel's front desk how to get to the hospital. Now that she was here, what was she going to do? She didn't know Kevin. Not really. He was a competent grown-up who didn't need her checking on him and probably wouldn't appreciate her visit.

She crossed to the door and nearly left, then turned back and walked the length of the room. Okay, she was here. The nurse said she could see him in a few minutes. She would go into his room, thank him for the previous night and duck out while she still had some small measure of dignity.

"Are you here to see Kevin Harmon?"

Haley turned toward the speaker and saw a nurse standing in the doorway.

"Yes." Haley approached the woman. "Is he all right?"

"Actually he's doing surprisingly well, for a man who was shot." She smiled. "He's in Room 247. Right down at the end of the hall."

"Thanks."

Haley clutched her purse to her stomach and headed down the hall. As she walked, she tried to figure out what exactly she was going to say. After "Hi," her brain sort of stalled. She supposed she could pretend he was just another sick parishioner. She'd visited hundreds of them over the years.

Yes, that was it. She would think of Kevin as just one more member of her father's congregation. Not the man who had rescued her and then turned down her offer of carnal knowledge of her person.

The hospital door stood open. Haley knocked softly as she entered. There was only one bed in the room. The man in it turned his head as she entered, giving her a clear view of his face. Her feelings of concern turned to dread as she took in his bruised face and the bandage around his head. Where it wasn't bruised, his skin was pale in contrast to his thick, dark hair. His eyes were only partially open. One leg was propped up on a pillow and a thick bandage encircled his thigh.

"Kevin?"

He managed a slight smile. "You should see the other guy."

She bit her lower lip as she approached. "You look really beat up. How do you feel?"

"Like I was shot."

"I saw you being taken away on television. That's how I found out what happened."

"Thanks for visiting." He motioned to a straight-back chair against the wall. "Take a load off."

She pulled the chair closer and settled next to him. Without thinking, she took his hand in hers and squeezed. His fingers were warm and strong, and more than a little distracting.

"Is there anything I can do to help?"

His mouth curved up again. "Yeah. Don't talk to me about being fruit."

She remembered bits and pieces of their conversation of last night, when she'd wanted to be forbidden fruit. Embarrassment flooded her, making her cheeks burn. She quickly dropped his hand and stared at the floor.

"Yes...well, I wasn't exactly myself."

"For what it's worth, I liked whoever you were."

She raised her head and stared at him. "Really?"

"Absolutely."

"But I was an idiot."

"You were charming."

"I was drunk."

"A charming drunk."

Their eyes locked. Despite the bruising and the bandage, Haley found herself getting lost in his gaze. Her insides shivered slightly. Her heart beat faster. A strange, unexpected yearning filled her and while she couldn't say for what, she ached with need.

The powerful sensation frightened her, so she did her best to ignore it. She forced herself to look away from Kevin's face. Instead, she focused on the bandage around his head.

"Was the riot the reason you were paged last night?" she asked.

"Yeah. They knew I was still in the area. All available personnel were summoned. By the time I got there, the riot had already turned dangerous."

"What started it?"

"It seems the prisoner I delivered yesterday had a lot of enemies in residence. A few of them got together and tried to kill him. They jumped a guard and took his gun." He touched his injured leg. "I got caught in the cross fire. Just dumb luck."

Haley didn't know what to say. Kevin spoke matter-of-factly, as if this sort of thing happened every day. "Have you ever been shot before?" she asked.

"Nope. And let me tell you, it hurts like a sonofa—" He caught himself and grinned. "It hurts a lot."

"You can swear. I don't mind. In fact, I plan on learning to swear."

"You're kidding."

She shook her head. "I don't want to do it a lot and there are some words I'm not interested in using. Once I learn to do it, then I can figure out if I like it or not. I was thinking of mostly the D-word or the H-word."

Kevin closed his eyes. "I've never heard anyone call it 'the D-word' before."

"I can't actually say it here."

He opened one eye. "In my room?"

"I'm in a hospital."

"That's not exactly like being in church."

"I know, but serious things happen here. Sometimes people die."

He opened his other eye. "You can't swear where people are dying?"

"No. Death is a sacred experience."

He rubbed his forehead. "You're from another planet, aren't you?"

"Sometimes it feels like I am," she admitted, thinking how different her world was from his. "I did very well in my classes at college, but none of them prepared me for this sort of thing."

"Are we talking about swearing or prison riots."

"Both."

"Uh-huh." He closed his eyes again.

She took the opportunity to study him. Even with his injuries, he was a tough-looking man. She supposed he should have frightened her, but he didn't. She knew that underneath the power and muscles beat a good and noble heart. He wasn't the kind of man to take advantage of a defenseless woman. Which was just her bad luck.

"How long will they keep you in the hospital?" she asked.

"Overnight. They want to make sure my head injury isn't serious. Somebody nailed me with a metal chair. I ducked, but not fast enough." He fingered the bandage. "There's some bruising around my inner ear, so I'm a little wobbly."

After last night, she knew the feeling.

"What about your leg?"

"It was a clean shot. Through the meat. It'll need regular changing, but it's just a matter of letting it heal."

He'd spoken without opening his eyes. Haley had the feeling that he was getting tired. She knew she should go and let him rest, but first she had to thank him for all that he'd done for her. And apologize.

"Kevin, I—"

A faint ringing interrupted her. He opened his eyes.

"Dammit, that's my cell phone," he mumbled, turning his head toward the sound. "It's in my jacket pocket. Probably in the closet. Would you get it?"

"Sure."

She rose and crossed to the small closet. As she opened the door, the ringing got louder. She pulled the phone out of his chest pocket and carried it to him. Kevin pushed a button.

"Harmon," he said, his voice brisk and all business.

A little shiver went through her. He was competent, she thought. So in charge. Not like any man she'd ever met, certainly nothing like Allan.

She crossed to the window and tried not to listen, but when he chuckled and said, "Hi, Mom," she couldn't help tuning in to the conversation.

She wouldn't have thought of him as someone with a mother. Not that she'd assumed he'd hatched from under a rock or anything, but for him to have a family meant he was just like everyone else. But now that she thought about it, she remembered him mentioning a brother. That part of last night was still a little blurry.

"Nothing much," he said, his words filled with warmth and affection.

Haley recognized the emotions and they warmed her. She liked that Kevin cared about his mother. Some people didn't get along with their folks. She'd never understood that. Didn't parents always do their best?

Her own father sometimes made her crazy, but she knew every action was motivated by love. Her need to get away wasn't about her father—at least not completely. There was also Allan, and her need to grow up and be independent.

"No, I'm okay," Kevin was saying. "What? I'm in the hospital. I was shot."

Haley couldn't help glancing over her shoulder at him. He held the phone away from his ear and gave her an "aren't parents a pain, even though we love them" look that made her feel as though she was part of the in crowd.

The momentary connection lightened her spirits. She'd never felt it with a man before. She'd thought that sort of thing only happened with girlfriends. It had certainly never happened with Allan, but a lot of things hadn't happened with him.

"No, you don't have to come get me," Kevin said. "I'll be fine. Yes, I'll be home in a couple of days. You're sure it's not an emergency, Mom? Promise?"

He listened for a couple of minutes, then sighed. "Mom, you don't have to worry. No, they don't think I'll have a limp, but I'll have a scar and you know how chicks go for scars."

Haley turned her attention back to the window and tried not to think about the scar on Kevin's leg. Would she find it attractive? She was female, but she'd never thought of herself as a chick.

"Okay. I'll keep you informed. I love you, too. 'Bye, Mom."

She heard a high-pitched *beep* as he disconnected the call.

"How did she take it?" she asked, turning back to face him.

"Not bad, considering. She's distracted. Apparently a family situation has come up in the past couple of days."

"What does that mean?"

"Hell if I know. She says it's not an emergency, but she also told me we have to talk. What is it about women and conversation?"

Haley was momentarily distracted by his easy use of the H-word. It took her a second to respond to his question.

"Men have conversations, too."

"Maybe, but we never start them with the words 'we have to talk.'" He shuddered. "Four of the most frightening words in the English language."

She laughed. "Why?"

"Because they usually mean the guy has screwed up somewhere. He's in big trouble and she's about to tell him everything he's going to have to do to make it right. Who wants to hear that?"

"I see your point," she said, which reminded her of her own. She crossed to the bed.

"I don't want to stay too long. I know you need your rest. But I did want to thank you for last night."

He brushed aside her comment with a wave of his hand. "No big deal."

"It was to me. You were very considerate and I appreciate that." She clutched her purse tightly in both hands. "I'd never been drunk before."

"No kidding."

She shifted her weight from foot to foot. "I didn't really mean for that to happen."

"I don't buy that for a second, Haley. You were ordering margaritas, so you meant for something to happen."

"I guess you're right." She circled the bed and sank down into the chair. "Life is very confusing right now. I have a lot of decisions to make about my life. I thought the drive would give me time to think things through."

"Long drives always work for me." He smiled at her. "It's only been a couple of days. Give yourself a break. You'll get it figured out."

His faith in her made her smile. "Thanks. What about you? What are you going to do?"

"First, take advantage of the very generous hospitality here. I'm off duty until I'm cleared by the doctor. It could be three or four weeks."

"Will you go home?"

"As soon as I can."

"Do you want me to take you to the airport?"

He shook his head, then winced and touched the bandage. "You don't have to stick around for me. Besides, I'm not flying home."

"Why not?"

He pointed to his bandaged ear. "Until the swelling goes down, I'm not allowed in the air. Something about pressure and elevation."

She glanced at his injured leg. "So how will you get there?"

"Drive."

"How?"

"I'll wait until I'm well enough."

Haley didn't know that much about gunshot wounds, but she didn't think they healed all that quickly. Not when the bullet had gone all the way through his leg.

A thought occurred to her. It wasn't as if she had an appointment or anything. Driving was driving. So what if she got to California a few days late? She could offer to take him home.

She glanced at him, then away. Maybe that wasn't a good idea. Kevin had been really nice and everything, but he obviously didn't find her attractive. Would he want to spend that much time in her company? Still, she owed him. She should at least offer. It was the right thing to do.

What she refused to acknowledge, even to herself, was the sense that she didn't want to say goodbye. There was something about being around him that made her feel good about herself.

"I've taken several first-aid classes," she said cautiously. "We offer them at the church and in the past couple of years, I've been teaching them. So I have some basic first-aid knowledge."

He watched her without speaking. Haley cleared her throat.

"My point is, I could probably change your bandage."

"Thanks, but if I can't do it myself, I'll just make my way to the hospital."

"I didn't mean I would stay here. I was offering to drive you home."

It seemed that he was still inviting trouble into his

life, Kevin thought as Haley spoke. She detailed all the reasons it made sense for her to help him, concluding with, "I owe you for last night. For not, um, well, taking advantage of me."

The last couple of words came out as a mumble. She ducked her head and he could barely make out what she was saying. Still, it was enough for him to remember helping her back to her room. Even drunk and practically incoherent, she'd been appealing. Too appealing.

There was no way he could spend that much time with her. Shot or not, even with his head pounding, even with her in another hideous floral-print dress that looked more like a tent than a fashion statement, he wanted her. Yup, right here under the scratchy sheet, with the painkiller coursing through his veins, his groin throbbed with an ache that had nothing to do with recent injuries.

Spending time with Haley, even the day or two it would take to get to Possum Landing, would be a level of torture he didn't deserve.

She was too sweet, too innocent, too...everything. She deserved way more than the likes of him.

"I don't want to hold you up," he said, trying to sound gentle instead of horny. "Don't you have an island to drive to?"

She smiled slightly. "I already told you, I know I can't drive to Hawaii."

She looked at him. Despite being a grown woman, she obviously didn't know how to conceal what she was thinking. He could see every thought flashing through her big eyes. Hope, fear, excitement. He made her nervous, but he could see she still wanted him to say yes. For reasons that weren't clear to him, she wanted to spend time in his company.

Why? Did she see him as some knight who had come to her rescue?

"I'm not one of the good guys," he told her, angry at her for thinking the best of him and angry at himself for caring.

She frowned. "Of course you are. You're a U.S. Marshal. And last night—"

"Just forget about that. It doesn't count."

"It does to me."

Trouble, he thought again. She *was* trouble, he was *in* trouble and damn if it wasn't going to get worse.

He shouldn't say yes, but he couldn't say no. Somehow he'd been trapped.

Last night, she'd wanted him to kiss her. If she hadn't been drunk, he would have obliged. Then what would have happened? Stupid question. He already knew the answer.

If he wasn't strong enough to turn down her offer to drive him home, how was he going to resist anything else she might choose to throw his way?

"Be careful what you wish for," he told her. "You just might get it. And then where will you be?"

Haley blinked at him. "Was that a yes?"

He was slime. Actually, he was the single-celled creatures that aspired to be slime. He was going to hell for sure.

"Yes."

Chapter Four

The next day, despite several protests and some muttered grumbling, Kevin found himself being wheeled
out of the hospital. The practice of forcing patients to
leave via wheelchair didn't make sense to him. The
second he was gone, he would be on his own and
expected to walk, so why not now?

The drill-sergeant-looking nurse hadn't been impressed by his argument.

But his mild humiliation and annoyance were instantly forgotten when he was wheeled out in front of
the main building and saw Haley waiting for him.
Sure he noticed her—she had on yet another of her
incredibly ugly shapeless dresses that fell nearly to
her ankles and covered her arms down to the elbow.
Somewhere underneath the faded-purple, floral-print
fabric was a great body, not that anyone could tell by

looking. Yet it wasn't Haley that captured his attention. Instead, it was her car.

He was a typical guy with some interest in cars. Faster was always better than slower. Sleek was a nice bonus. Haley was a conservative young woman from a small town. He would have guessed she drove a sensible sedan of some kind. Nothing flashy. Nothing outrageous. He could never have put her with the massive pale yellow Cadillac convertible she stood next to.

It had stopped raining at some point between his being shot and now, which was a good thing because the top was down.

He shook his head to clear his vision—obviously this was an illusion—then wished he hadn't when pain exploded behind his eyes. When he could speak without wincing, he squinted slightly and told her, "This can't be your car."

She beamed. Really. It was like looking into the sun. "Isn't it fabulous? Don't you love it?" She opened the passenger door and stroked the buff-colored leather. Not exactly a practical color.

"I traded my car in for this. There's no way you would have fit in my old car. Not with your leg and all. I saw this on the lot and fell in love. I've never felt this way about a car before. It's spectacular."

He wasn't sure if she meant the vehicle or her feelings for it, then he decided he didn't want to know. "How much did you pay?"

"Oh, I got a great deal."

"Uh-huh." Somehow he wasn't convinced.

The nurse helped him to his feet. He shifted his

weight, took a single step and slid onto the smooth leather. He had to admit it was certainly big enough. With the passenger seat all the way back, he could stretch out his injured leg and still have room to spare.

"Thanks," Haley said to the nurse, then took the paper sack holding Kevin's belongings from her and tossed it into the back seat. She shut his door and walked around to the driver's side.

"This is going to be so great," she said when she'd settled into her seat. "I stopped and got maps. I have our route all figured out. It took me a while to find Possum Landing, but then I did. A mechanic checked out the car for me and swears it won't be any trouble at all."

Kevin squinted against the sun and wished he had his sunglasses, or at least a hat to protect him from the glare. The late morning was warm. At least the heat felt good.

"You don't even know where we are. How did you find a mechanic?"

"I called a local church and asked the minister's secretary to recommend one. When I explained the problem, she said her brother was a mechanic and that he would be happy to help. He even came with me to the dealer."

Smart move, he conceded. Maybe she hadn't been robbed. "You've had a busy morning."

"I had fun." She started the engine. "We need to go by your motel and get your things. I'm all checked out and packed. Then we can head out. I figure it will take us four days to get to Possum Landing."

Kevin leaned his aching head against the headrest

and closed his eyes. Three seconds later they popped open. "Four days? It can't be more than six or seven hundred miles." They could practically do that in a day.

"I know." Haley put the car in drive and headed out of the parking lot. "I like to go about two hundred miles a day. There are so many wonderful things to see."

He closed his eyes again. "Like what?" he asked, already sure he didn't want to know.

"Little out-of-the-way towns, museums, antique shops. I've had the best time exploring the country since I left Ohio. You meet the most interesting people."

How could he argue with that? He'd met her.

"Four days, huh?"

"It will be fun," she promised.

Maybe. Maybe not. He figured he could have stayed put, healed in a motel and been able to drive home in about the same amount of time it was going to take Haley to deliver him.

"Oh." She glanced at him, her smile fading. "I forgot. You need to get home quickly. You have that family thing going on."

She was wearing sunglasses, but he could imagine the light fading from her eyes. He remembered his mother's promise that everything was fine and what she had to discuss with him wouldn't go anywhere. She'd said it wasn't about anyone being sick or dying. As she'd never lied to him in the past, he had no reason to doubt her now.

"It's not an emergency," he said before he could stop himself. "We don't have to rush."

"Really?"

The smile returned and when it did, something inside him sparked to life. He didn't want to know what it was, or what it all meant. Just his luck, he was going to be trapped in a car with Haley for several days. While his injuries distracted him now, what would happen when he started to heal and found himself wanting her? Did he have enough self-control to do the right thing?

Hell of a way to find out, he thought as he closed his eyes again and tried to relax. Beside him, Haley turned on the radio. "Pink Cadillac" was playing. Wouldn't you just know it?

Haley drove to the row of motels by the bar where she and Kevin had first met. He directed her to the plain two-story building where he'd rented a room. She found a parking place right in front, turned off the engine, then circled around the car to help him to his feet.

"I'm fine," Kevin protested as she swung open the passenger door.

She reached into the back and handed him the cane he'd been given in the hospital. He used it to push himself slowly to his feet. Once there, he wobbled a bit. She moved close and started to put an arm around his waist.

"I'll be okay," he said, and took a step toward the motel door.

As Haley watched, some of the color seemed to

drain from his face, leaving behind pale skin and multiple purple-and-red bruises. They'd removed the bandage from around his head. The bandage on his thigh was still in place. It was thick and very white against his skin where someone had cut the right leg of his jeans off just below the crotch to get them over the bandage.

"You look like you're going to fall over," she said, trying not to sound too worried. "I don't think I can pick you up on my own."

He glanced at her and almost smiled. "Thanks for the news flash. I'll keep it in mind."

He took small, halting steps toward the motel door, then fished the key out of his jeans' pocket. Haley grabbed the bag of his belongings from the back seat and followed him into the small room.

The space wasn't all that different from the room she'd had. Full-size bed, TV, a small dresser and a bathroom off to one side. Kevin sank onto the only chair in the room and sucked in a breath.

"Okay, maybe crutches would have been a better idea."

She studied the sweat on his face. "We could go back to the hospital and get them."

He shook his head. "By tomorrow I'll be fine."

She had her doubts, but didn't say anything. He was trying to act tough, but he wasn't doing a very good job of it. No doubt getting hit in the head and shot took a lot out of a man. If she'd been the one in his position, she would have refused to leave her hospital bed for a least a week.

He jerked his head toward the small closet. "My overnight bag is in there."

She crossed to the louvered door and pulled it open. A black duffel bag sat on the carpeted floor. "Is this it?" she asked.

"I was only planning to spend the night."

She thought about the three suitcases of her belongings that were currently in her trunk. Of course she hadn't had much of a plan when she'd decided to run for freedom, so she'd pretty much packed all her clothes.

She set the empty duffel on the bed and went into the bathroom first. An electric shaver, can of deodorant, toothbrush and toothpaste and a brush and comb sat on the small glass shelf. Haley put them into the black zip-up container sitting on the back of the toilet, then checked the shower for shampoo. There was only a small bottle provided by the motel.

She returned to the bedroom and tucked the shaving kit into the duffel, then turned her attention to the paper sack from the hospital.

His jacket was inside. The garment had been rolled up. When she shook it out, something hard, dark and scary fell onto the bed.

A gun.

Haley jumped back as if she'd been bitten by a snake.

Despite his battered appearance, Kevin managed a low chuckle. "Don't panic. The safety's on."

"How do you know?"

"I checked it myself. Bring it here and I'll show you."

Bring it? As in, pick it up and carry it? Haley sucked in a breath, then very carefully picked up the gun. It was cold and heavier than it looked. She crossed to where Kevin was sitting. He took it from her and pointed to a small lever.

"See how it's down?"

She nodded.

"That means the safety is on. It won't go off."

"Is it loaded?"

"Yes."

She'd never seen a gun before, not in the flesh, so to speak. And certainly not one that was loaded. She and Kevin were not from the same place at all, she thought.

She eyed the deadly weapon. "Have you ever killed anyone?" she asked without thinking.

The silence in the room grew, pushing against her until she wanted to drag the words back and never even think the question. Kevin tossed the gun onto the bed and rubbed the bridge of his nose.

"Don't ask questions unless you want the answer," he told her.

Haley sucked in a breath. He glanced at her and in that second she saw the truth in his eyes. He *had* killed someone. She saw the flicker of ghosts, the echo of pain.

"Rethinking your invitation to drive me home?" he asked wryly.

"Of course not. You'd never hurt me. Whoever you shot deserved it."

"You sound sure of yourself."

"I am."

"Does anyone deserve to die that way?"

"Did you have a choice?"

"No."

"That's good enough for me."

She walked to the dresser, but before she could pull out a drawer he spoke her name. She turned to him.

"Just like that?" he asked. "You're not curious, not worried?"

"You said you didn't have a choice. I believe you."

His dark eyes narrowed. "I could be lying."

"You're not."

"Maybe trusting me isn't such a good idea."

That made her smile. "The fact that you're trying to warn me about yourself only reinforces my point." She pulled out the dresser drawer and froze.

Logically she'd known she was helping him pack his clothes. That's why she was here. So it made sense that she would be seeing his clothes, even touching them as she put them into his duffel. But knowing and doing it were two different things.

She stared at the neatly folded pair of briefs—dark blue briefs—and the clean socks. But it was the underwear that caught her attention. She'd never seen a man's underwear before. Well, okay, she'd seen her father's on occasion, although the housekeeper usually did the laundry. Her father wore plain white boxer shorts. Not dark blue briefs.

"Everything all right?" Kevin asked.

She nodded without speaking, then scooped up the garments and tossed them into the bag. In the next drawer down was a clean T-shirt. There weren't any other clothes.

"I hadn't planned on an extended trip," he said when she straightened. "I guess we should stop somewhere and get me a few things. I remember there being a Wal-Mart store just off the highway. That should work."

"You don't have any pajamas."

He grinned. "Never bother with 'em."

"Oh."

So what did he sleep in? His clothes? No, that didn't make sense. His—

"Nothing."

She looked at him and blinked. "Excuse me?"

"You were wondering what I slept in. I told you. Nothing. I sleep naked."

The N-word. Heat flared instantly and she pressed her hands to her cheeks.

"You've got to get out more," he told her, chuckling.

She dropped her hands to her sides and nodded. "I guess so."

Naked. She didn't want to think about it. She didn't want to think about anything else. What would it be like to be so comfortable with herself and her body that she would be able to sleep without clothes? She couldn't imagine that happening.

It only took a few more minutes for her to double check the room, then help Kevin back to the car. She put his half-full duffel in the trunk, then returned the room key to the front desk.

He directed her toward the Wal-Mart. As she drove

she couldn't help thinking about his colored briefs and the fact that he slept naked and that last night she'd wanted him to kiss her. He'd refused, but for a second, she'd wondered if he'd been tempted. Maybe if she hadn't thrown up he would have done it. And then what? Would things have progressed?

She glanced at him sitting next to her and knew that she wouldn't have protested. Even beat-up Kevin looked good. Last night he'd been…delicious.

She smiled slightly. No man had ever fit that description before, but he did. And she knew that he would never have pushed her too far. He wouldn't have made her feel uncomfortable and she would bet that he would have been a really good kisser. In fact, despite the bruises and the bullet wound, she still wanted to kiss him. Very much.

But she wouldn't say anything. Mostly because without the courage brought on by margaritas, thinking about it wasn't nearly as rough as actually convincing him to do it. Still, they were going to be together for several days. Who knew what could happen in all that time?

The sight of the Wal-Mart up ahead broke through her musings. She made a mental note to fantasize about Kevin another time and pulled into the parking lot.

She was lucky enough to find a spot up front, which meant Kevin didn't have to hobble very far. When she'd settled him into a seat at the snack bar, she sat across from him and pulled a piece of paper out of her purse.

"We'll need supplies for changing your bandage," she said, and started writing.

"New jeans," he said. "The bandage will be smaller in a couple of days and regular jeans will fit. Thirty-four waist, thirty-six inseam."

Haley scribbled the numbers down, not sure what they meant. But she hoped she would figure it out when she hit the men's department.

"Socks, briefs. Plain white is fine."

She glanced at him and saw humor brightening his eyes. So he *had* noticed her embarrassment when she'd seen his underwear.

"Maybe a couple of shirts?" she asked, trying to act as though this was no big deal.

"Yeah, but nothing fancy. T-shirts, polo shirts, whatever."

"Okay. I'll turn your pain-medicine prescription in first and pick it up when I'm done. You're going to want to stay here, right?"

He nodded. "I'm not feeling strong enough to walk the aisles and I'm too big to be pushed around in a cart."

She smiled. "Do you want something to eat or drink?"

"Maybe some water."

She got him a bottle of water and a pretzel from the attendant at the snack bar, then collected a cart for herself and headed out.

After turning in the prescription and collecting the medical supplies she would need, she walked back to the men's department. She went for easy first, and perused the jeans. Kevin's size information instantly

made sense and she collected a pair to fit his speci-
fications. They were new and a little stiff, so she made
a mental note to do laundry tonight when they
stopped.

Next up were shirts. She bought three, two short-
sleeved T-shirts in bright colors and a light blue polo
shirt. Underwear was next. Haley felt her face flame
as she pushed her cart into the rows of packaged
briefs and boxer shorts. She grabbed two sets of three
pairs, a bag of socks, and nearly ran toward the main
aisle. A quick glance at her watch told her she had
another fifteen minutes until the prescription would
be ready.

She turned to go back to the snack bar, but slowed
as she entered the women's department. It was June
and the aisles were filled with light, pretty summer
clothes. There were sleeveless shirts, floral print
skirts, T-shirts and shorts.

She stopped at a rack of shorts and fingered the
light cotton material. As if it had happened yesterday,
she remembered her eleventh birthday. She'd had a
great party with lots of friends, but when it was over,
two of the mothers had stayed to talk to her. They'd
carefully explained that she was going to be devel-
oping into a young woman soon, and young women
dressed appropriately. It wouldn't do for the minister's daughter to be seen showing off her body.

At first, Haley hadn't understood, but eventually
everything had been made clear. Shorts and shirts had
been replaced by loose-fitting summer dresses that
made her feel ugly. She'd been unable to climb trees
or to even ride her bike. On her eleventh birthday

she'd gone from being a kid to being a young lady, and she'd hated it.

Haley glanced down at her loose-fitting dress. It was sensible and not the least bit revealing. Allan had loved it. Then she turned her attention to cute summer clothes all around her. There were dozens of styles of shorts, with matching tops, and even cute little summer sweaters. She grabbed several of each in her size and moved toward the dressing room. On her way she picked up a sleeveless summer dress that would skim her curves, then came to stop in front of a display of feminine nighties and pj sets.

She picked out a light blue camisole with matching tap pants and a short nightgown with skinny straps and an appliqué declaring the wearer Queen of Everything.

Right in front of the dressing room was the lingerie. Haley stared at colored bras with matching bikini panties. There were bright colors and pastels, cotton, satin, nylon and—she gasped—animal prints. No plain white utilitarian undergarments in sight.

Instantly her conscience started telling her that she wasn't that kind of girl. Could she really see herself in a tiger print bra and matching panty?

"But I want to be that kind of girl," she murmured, and scooped up one of everything in her size.

After a flurry of activity in the dressing room, Haley settled on a week's worth of lingerie, three different styles of pj's, four pair of shorts with shirts for each, two sundresses that had nothing to do with the ugly garments she usually wore when it was warm, jeans and a denim skirt that didn't come close to touching her knees.

On her way to pick up Kevin's prescription she detoured through shoes and found a pair of strappy sandals and some white athletic shoes imprinted with rhinestone flowers. She couldn't wait to get settled for the night to try on all her clothes again. Haley tried to remember the last time she'd been this happy, but no event came to mind. Maybe running away *had* been the right thing to do.

Kevin finished his bottle of water, ignored the pretzel and wished for a double dose of pain medicine. Every part of him hurt, even his hair. He couldn't tell how long Haley had been gone, but he sure as hell wished she would come back so they could leave.

Before he could figure out a way to have her paged, she appeared in front of him, pushing a cart overflowing with plastic bags.

"What did you buy?" he asked as he struggled to his feet.

"Just a few things." She was instantly at his side, helping him get upright, then supporting him.

"You look awful," she told him as they slowly made their way out of the store.

"Good. I feel awful. I like the two to match."

"Wait here."

She left him propped against the building and brought the car right up front, then eased him into the passenger seat. The world blurred a little as he leaned his head back.

He heard her putting away bags, then the driver's door slammed shut. The sound made his head ache more.

"You need to rest," she said as she placed her cool hand on his bruised cheek. "I'm going to get us a room for the night."

He thought about protesting. It wasn't even two in the afternoon and at her rate of travel, they couldn't afford to lose a day. But the thought of driving anywhere was impossible. Right now he just wanted something to take away the pain and he wanted to sleep.

"Here."

She pressed something into his hand. He opened one eye and saw a pill resting on his palm. She offered him a bottle of water. He downed the medicine and handed her back the bottle. She'd read his mind. He would have thought that was a bad quality in a woman, but in Haley's case, he was willing to make an exception.

"Don't worry," she said as she started the engine. "I'll take care of everything."

He thought about protesting that she couldn't take care of herself let alone someone else, but he couldn't form the words. Besides, there was a part of him that was willing to put his fate in Haley's small hands. Crazy, but true.

He might have dozed or just passed out. Sometime later, he felt Haley lightly touching his shoulder. He opened his eyes and saw that they were parked in front of a motel. At least it isn't pink, he thought, just coherent enough to be grateful.

Haley helped him to his feet, then led him into the

room. She didn't look all that strong, but she didn't seem to be crumbling under his weight.

"You need to eat," she said as she opened the door and eased him inside. "But you should probably rest first."

She was taking care of him. Kevin tried to remember the last time that had happened. It had been years—maybe before he'd screwed up for the last time at home and had been sent to military school. If he remembered right, he'd stolen old man Miller's car. It had been a Caddy, too.

He chuckled at the similarity.

"What's so funny?" Haley asked.

"Just my past catching up with me."

"Let it catch up with you in bed. Here you go."

She stopped beside the bed and let him fall into a sitting position. Even as he collapsed back, she was shifting his legs so he was stretched out on the mattress.

Haley sat next to him and once again put her cool hand on his face. He liked her touching him. In any other circumstances, he would have asked her to touch a little lower. But things being as they were, he simply opened his eyes and gazed at her.

"I was afraid to leave you on your own for the night," she said, her blue-hazel eyes wide and serious-looking. "So we're sharing a room. I hope that's okay."

He turned his head just enough to see the other bed. "Fine by me," he rasped, feeling the pain medicine kick in. The edge came off his hurt and he was getting sleepy.

"I don't want you to think—" she began, then stopped.

"Right now, I'm not thinking at all. If you're expecting any action, kid, you're gonna have to come and get it because I'm not gonna be good for squat tonight."

He heard her suck in a breath and her cheeks might have been turning red, but things were starting to blur. He had one last coherent thought, and that was that she had a very kissable mouth. Then the room shifted once and everything went black.

Chapter Five

Kevin woke to a wonderful smell. He opened his eyes and saw Haley setting out a dinner of fried chicken, coleslaw, corn and mashed potatoes on the small table by the window overlooking the parking lot. His stomach instantly cramped in anticipation of food. As he hadn't had much more than cereal in the hospital, he had a bad feeling that his last real meal had been the burger in the bar, nearly forty-eight hours before.

He pushed himself into a sitting position, was pleased that he only got a little dizzy, then lowered his feet to the floor. That movement sent a razor-sharp pain of protest through his thigh, but he ignored it.

"I hope you got plenty," he said, returning his attention to Haley. "Because I'm—"

Starved. That was the next word in the sentence.

He knew it and he couldn't say it. He doubted he could say anything. Ever again.

She glanced over and smiled at him. "You look a lot better than you did. You were out for nearly three hours. I guess you needed to rest. I broke my arm once, when I was little. It hurt a lot and I know I always felt better after sleeping. Not that a broken arm is anything like getting shot. Well, maybe it is. I don't know." She paused for breath and frowned. "Kevin? Are you all right?"

He was. At least he would be when consciousness returned. But until then he'd stepped into an alternative universe. Or hell. That was it. He'd died and this was hell. It couldn't be heaven because there was no way God would approve of what Haley was wearing.

Logically, Kevin knew that in warm weather women dressed in things like T-shirts and shorts. It was common. Expected even. He agreed, in theory. Just not Haley. She wore shapeless ugly dresses that covered her body like a shroud. She would never put on a tiny white T-shirt that barely came down to the middle of her rib cage and she would never be caught dead in tiny white shorts that settled low enough on her hips to expose her flat stomach and her delicate belly button. Would she?

"What the hell are you wearing?" he demanded, the words coming out a little more forcefully than he'd intended.

Haley jumped and set down the container of chicken. She glanced at herself, then back at him.

"Clothes."

He had a feeling she was doing her best to sound

defiant. She didn't come close, but he gave her points for trying.

"What happened to your dress?"

"Nothing, except I hate it. I haven't worn shorts since I turned eleven. I figured it was long past time."

She pulled a quart of milk out of an ice bucket on the floor and poured them each a glass. As she bent to reach the far side of the small table, the T-shirt not only rode up a little, it gaped at her neckline and he could see down the front to the swell of her breasts and the white lace of her bra.

Desire and pain seemed to be battling it out. He was curious as to which would win.

She glanced at him out of the corner of her eye. Something about the set of her mouth and the tension in her shoulders told him she was expecting him not to approve. Kevin knew all about disappointing those who mattered most, and trying to balance between what was expected and what one really wanted. No way was he going to guilt Haley that way. Not on purpose anyway.

"You look nice," he said finally, and reached for his cane.

Haley was at his side in an instant and helped him to his feet. "Do you really think I look okay? This isn't too…brazen?"

Brazen? He held in a laugh. "If they sell it at Wal-Mart, it has to be all right."

"I hope so. I bought some other shorts and shirts, along with other things. While you were sleeping, I washed everything, including your jeans. They're not so stiff now."

As she spoke, she put her arm around his waist and led him to the table. He could feel her breast brushing again his side and he inhaled the sweet scent of her body. Speaking of stiff, he thought and sighed. In the battle of pain and desire, it seemed that baser instincts were going to win. He shouldn't even be surprised.

"I appreciate you doing the laundry," he said when he was at the table. "You got yourself into more than you bargained for by offering to drive me home."

She sat opposite him and picked up a napkin. "I don't mind. This is fun. If I were home I would be—" She stopped talking and pressed her full lips together.

"What would you be doing?"

"Nothing interesting."

"If you call driving me around and doing my laundry interesting, then you were right to run away."

She laughed. "You have a point. If nothing else, the motel has great cable."

"Aren't minister's daughters allowed to watch cable at home?"

"Sure, but there isn't much time for leisure activities."

"What sort of leisure activities *was* there time for?"

Haley took a bite of chicken and chewed slowly. Kevin couldn't help wondering if she was just being polite or stalling for an answer.

"I don't mean to make my life sound horrible," she said at last. "My father is a wonderful man who loves me very much."

"I don't doubt that. But sometimes it's hard living with a lot of expectations and rules."

Her eyebrows pulled together. "It is for me."

"Me, too." He shrugged. "My brother was always the perfect kid and I was always the one getting into trouble. I was forever getting grounded, then sneaking out, getting caught and being grounded again."

Haley nibbled on her coleslaw. "I never got in trouble at all. Sometimes I felt like I couldn't even think a bad thought without someone figuring it out."

"That would have been tough," he said. "I'm the kid who brought a box of cockroaches to school when I was seven and let 'em loose."

She stared at him. "You didn't."

He made an X over his chest. "Cross my heart."

"What happened?"

"There was a lot of screaming. I had detention for about six years. At least it felt that long."

She smiled. "I never had detention."

"It's not as fun as it sounds."

"I guess not. What else did you do?"

He wasn't sure if her curiosity about his checkered past was good or bad. "I got two of my friends drunk when we were nine, got caught shoplifting when I was fourteen. That was my first arrest. The first girl I kissed was fifteen and I was twelve and the first woman I ever—"

The self-editing switch kicked in just in time. Haley leaned forward. "Don't stop there."

He caught himself before he shook his head. There was no need to tempt fate with movements designed to leave him in agony. Besides, his loose lips had already gotten him into enough trouble.

"Let's just say she was an older woman."

"How old?"

"Nineteen."

"How old were you?"

He picked up an ear of corn. "This is a really great dinner."

"Kevin! How old?"

He sighed. "Fifteen."

She gasped. "You were fifteen the first time you ever…"

Her voice trailed off. Her expression hovered somewhere between horrified and impressed. He hoped she settled on the latter.

"I was a curious kid," he said.

"Obviously. And since then?"

He didn't catch the movement in time and shook his head. Instantly, pain exploded. He closed his eyes against it and when he opened them, he found her staring at him expectantly.

"No way," he told her. "I'm not getting into numbers."

"Can you give me a range?"

"Less than a hundred."

"More than ten?"

He sighed. "Yes."

"More than—"

"I'll tell you how many if you'll tell me what you're running away from."

As he suspected, that shut her up. She picked up

another piece of chicken and took a bite. "It's not anything bad."

He grinned. "Haley, I doubt you've ever done anything wrong in your life."

"You're right. Which is why this is the perfect time to start."

Just what he needed. "Do me a favor," he said. "Wait to start a life of being bad until you've dropped me off home. I don't want to be responsible for leading you astray."

"But wouldn't you be really good at it?"

"Probably the best. But I'm already on shaky ground where my redemption is concerned. Taking you over to the dark side would push me over the edge. You wouldn't want that on your conscience, would you?"

"I don't know. I'll have to think about."

Not exactly the answer he'd been hoping for.

Haley tried to concentrate on the cosmetics line being demonstrated on the television shopping channel. She'd never been one to wear much makeup and the skill required to line her upper lids had always eluded her, so the idea of a flat brush, almost like a mini paintbrush, to help with the application seemed sensible. Plus there were about a dozen color choices. She was leaning toward the dark purple, but then thought she might want to start with a more neutral brown or gray. Under other circumstances, she might have called and placed an order. Only two things stopped her.

The first was that she no longer had an actual address. She'd run away from home with no real destination in mind and she didn't plan on returning to her father's house anytime soon. The second problem was that she couldn't completely pay attention to the show. She was trying to, but at the same time she was listening intently for any sound coming from the bathroom.

Despite her protests, Kevin had insisted on taking a shower. She didn't think he should be standing for that long, nor was she sure he actually could. He'd sworn he would be fine and had even agreed to take his cane into the bathroom. At least there was a big bar in the shower, so he would have something to hold on to if he lost his balance. Still, she couldn't help worrying. If he fell, he could hurt himself even more than he already was. Plus, there was no way she was strong enough to lift him to safety.

So while the water ran, she tried to distract herself from her worry by watching TV. She'd already folded all the laundry she'd washed in the motel's machines. She'd put their new clothes away in the dresser drawers. The act had been oddly…intimate.

Funny how after all this time she was finally sharing a room with a man, and it was under circumstances she never could have imagined. She'd always assumed the first time she spent the night with a man, it would be after getting married. For the past several years, she'd pictured the man in question as Allan.

Kevin was about as different from Allan as it was possible for a man to be, which made the situation strange but not uncomfortable.

The water shut off. Haley half sat up, then flopped

back down on the bed and watched the model on television apply lip liner. Her thoughts about which color she liked best were interrupted by a loud groan, then a grunt. She tensed, but didn't move. They'd agreed she would wait out here until Kevin called her in to change his bandage.

After a few minutes, water ran again, followed by silence and a couple more groans. Finally, when she could barely stand it, the bathroom door opened.

She was on her feet in an instant. "Are you all right?"

"I'm still standing. The bandage is soaking, so it needs changing. You sure you're up to that?"

"Absolutely." Haley had already collected the first-aid supplies. She scooped them up into her arms and headed toward the bathroom.

"Brace yourself," Kevin said, pushing the door open wide. "I managed to pull on a T-shirt, but I'm not wearing pants."

"No problem."

Haley spoke the words casually, even though her heart was pounding hard enough to bruise a rib. She told herself that seeing Kevin in briefs and a T-shirt was just like going to the beach. Not that she'd been since she was a kid. Actually he would be wearing more. She would be fine.

She stepped into the small, steamy room. The air was scented with soap and shampoo. After setting the fresh bandages and antiseptic cream on the narrow counter by the sink, she reluctantly turned her attention to the man sitting on the edge of the tub.

As promised he'd pulled on a loose-fitting T-shirt.

He'd also draped a towel across his lap. She was both relieved and slightly curious about what he was covering up.

But this wasn't the time to deal with any of that. She sank to her knees and reached for scissors.

"Did you get dizzy? Does everything hurt?" she asked as she cut through the soaked bandage.

"Don't worry. The painkiller I took after dinner is kicking in."

"Which means you're dizzy but you don't care?"

He chuckled.

She glanced up and found herself getting lost in his brown eyes. He'd brushed his wet hair straight back. Two days' worth of stubble darkened his cheeks. He looked pretty darned good.

The bandage fell to the floor with a faint *thunk*. She pulled her attention from Kevin's face to his leg, then nearly fainted when she saw the raw wound from the gunshot.

"Haley? Are you going to pass out on me?"

Her stomach heaved once, but she ignored it. "I'm fine." It was only a white lie and shouldn't really count. She reached for the antiseptic cream and squeezed some on. Kevin's only reaction was to suck in his breath.

She worked quickly but gently. When the new bandage was secure, she rose and held out her arm.

"I'll help you into bed," she said.

He didn't protest, which told her how bad he was feeling. Together they made the short walk into the other room. She'd already pulled back the covers on his bed. He sat heavily, then shifted and stretched out on the mattress. Haley bent to grab the covers. But before she pulled them up she allowed herself one quick look.

Even with the bandage around his thigh, his legs looked powerful and long. His hips were narrow, his stomach flat. Broad shoulders pulled at the seams of his T-shirt. And his face—

When her gaze settled there, she realized he was watching her. Awareness brightened his eyes and turned up the corners of his mouth.

Horrified, she started to turn away, but he caught her wrist and held her in place.

"I don't mind you looking," he said, his voice low.

She kept her back to him. "I shouldn't have. You're injured."

"All the better to take advantage of me."

She spun back to face him. "I would never do that."

He chuckled. "I already figured that one out."

He released her and she pulled up the covers. When she would have stepped away, he patted the side of the bed.

"Have a seat."

She perched on the edge of the mattress, incredibly aware of her hip pressing against his body. He stunned her by taking her hand in his and lacing their fingers together. Heat filled her, making her breathing quicken. They were alone in a hotel room and he was holding her hand. How had she ever gotten so lucky?

"Tell me about the other men in your life," he said.

"What other men?"

"Yeah, that would be my point. Have you ever seen a man before?"

The question confused her. Of course she had. She could see him right now. Then she got it. Oh. "You mean—"

If he hadn't been holding her hand, she would have turned away.

"Naked, Haley. The word you're looking for is naked."

She stared at their fingers and at the way her wrist looked small and frail next to his. Instead of speaking an answer, she shook her head no.

"How did you get to the ripe old age of twenty-five without ever seeing a naked man?"

"They usually come to church with their clothes on." She risked glancing at him and saw him grin.

"Good point. Probably any boyfriends would worry about what your father would have to say if they flashed the goods."

Flashed the goods? She was both shocked and amused. Would Allan have ever said anything like that to her? She couldn't imagine it.

"The other night you said you'd only kissed three guys. Is that true?"

She nodded, caught up in the fact that they'd only met a couple of days before. Somehow she felt as if she'd known Kevin forever.

"That's not very many," he said. "How can you compare technique and style with a sample of three?"

"It's been a problem. I never knew if I kissed okay and I didn't know how to ask."

When she'd gotten drunk, she'd been hoping Kevin

would want to make it four and maybe give her some pointers, but he'd resisted her attempts to seduce him. It was just her luck to fall in with a gentleman.

"Haley, you don't have a clue as to what's going on, do you?"

"What are you talking about?"

"My point exactly."

He stared at her, his dark eyes seeming to see into her soul. His thumb brushed against the back of her hand in a way that left her more than a little breathless. The room seemed very quiet—she couldn't even hear the television.

"The thing is, with this painkiller, I'm pretty out of it."

"Sort of like me the other night."

"Exactly. So we're even."

She felt he was trying to tell her something, but she didn't know what.

"Do you want to kiss me?" he asked.

She would have thought she was done with her shocks for the day, but no. Here was yet another one. Blood rushed from her head to her feet, which made the room spin, then hurried back in place. She tried to breathe and couldn't. Tried to stand, but not a single muscle so much as twitched.

"It's not like I'm in a position to protest," he told her.

She didn't understand. "But you said you weren't interested."

"I'm pretty damn sure I never said that. My point was that *I* wouldn't do anything about it. That point still stands."

"So you don't want to kiss me?" Hurt flared in her chest. Then why had he brought it up?

"I'm not going to take advantage of you. That doesn't mean you're under the same constraints."

She blinked. Her mind heard the words, processed them and sent the results back.

She could kiss him.

"Oh." She blinked again. "Oh!"

Kiss a man? Her? As in, initiate? As in, start it? As in—

"I can hear you thinking from here."

She looked at his face, then narrowed her gaze to his mouth. "I've never kissed a man before."

"Maybe you'll like doing it."

Maybe she would.

Slowly, carefully, she leaned forward. At some point Kevin's eyes closed, which was good because she couldn't remember ever being this nervous before in her life and the last thing she wanted was him watching her. When she was almost there, she closed her eyes, too, because she wanted to feel everything. Then her lips brushed against his.

Her breath caught at the sweet, hot pressure. His mouth was firm yet yielding and felt exactly right against hers. She hovered there, not sure what to do. It had been years since she'd kissed anyone except Allan, and he'd always taken charge.

"Do whatever you want," Kevin murmured, once again reading her mind.

What did she want to do?

She pulled her hand free of his and gently touched his cheek. As she stroked his skin, she kissed him again, this time moving back and forth, pressing harder, then lighter, discovering possibilities. She found she liked being the one to kiss more, to pull back, to start again.

Tension swept through her body, making her legs tingle and her chest ache. The unfamiliar sensations forced her to lean closer. Kevin parted his lips in invitation and she didn't even hesitate before sweeping her tongue inside.

He tasted of minty toothpaste and something indescribably sweet. As they touched, fire seemed to leap between them. But the flames didn't burn. Instead, they pulled them closer together. He wrapped his arms around her, holding her against him. She could feel the pounding of his heart—somehow the rhythm matched her own.

She angled her head so they could kiss more deeply. They played and danced and circled and stroked. She wanted more. Funny how she wasn't clear on what that more might be, but she knew she wanted it. With Kevin. She trusted his strong hands to hold her and touch her. He would keep her safe on any journey.

She wasn't sure how long they kissed. Eventually the tingling in her thighs turned into something heavier and her breasts swelled uncomfortably in her new bra. Reluctantly, she sat up.

His eyes were dilated, his mouth swollen. They stared at each other without speaking. When he reached up and cupped her cheek with his palm, she turned her head to kiss his skin.

''You're full of surprises,'' he said, his voice low and husky.

She was a little surprised herself, but in a good way. She could feel her blood rushing through her body—reminding her of the pleasure of being alive. She'd just kissed a man for the first time ever. It had been great.

"Just for the record, you kiss fine."

"Maybe you should have kissed me last time I asked," she teased.

"No way. I wouldn't have stopped there."

"Really? You mean we would have—"

"Made love. A word of advice from someone who knows. Never do that when you're drunk."

His words made sense, but she would have to think about them another time. Right now she was too caught up in the concept of actually doing "it" with Kevin. Did that mean he wanted her? Was he aroused?

She didn't dare look and she couldn't ask. Did men get aroused just from kissing? What about making love? Did they—

He covered his ears. "Stop thinking so much."

He dropped his hands to his sides, then shifted and winced. She remembered his injuries.

"You'd better get some rest," she told him.

"Good idea. You going to be okay?"

"Uh-huh." Empowered by her recent experience, she bent and kissed his cheek. "Sleep well."

"I've created a monster," he muttered, closing his eyes. "You'd better not attack me in my sleep."

"I won't." But that didn't mean she wouldn't think about it.

Later that night, when Haley was sure that Kevin was asleep, she turned down the television and picked up the phone on the table between their beds. Using her newly purchased Wal-Mart calling card, she dialed the eight hundred number, entered her code, then the phone number for her father's office at the church. At this time of night the building would be deserted. She wouldn't have to worry about anyone picking up her call.

She listened to the four rings, followed by the answering machine message. When she heard the beep, she sucked in a breath and spoke quickly.

"Hi, Daddy. It's me. I wanted to call and let you know that I'm safe and well." She hesitated, not sure what else she should say. "I know you got my note, but that you'll still worry. I wish you wouldn't. I'm going to be okay. I just have to figure a few things out and I can't do that at home. I'm fine with Allan's decision. In fact I think he did the right thing. Please don't be too mad at him. I don't know how long I'll be gone. At least a few more weeks."

There was so much more she wanted to tell him, but not like this.

"I'll leave another message in a few days. I love you."

She hung up the phone. She didn't doubt that her father still cared about her. She was his daughter and nothing could make him stop loving her. But forgiving her was another matter entirely.

Chapter Six

They were on the road by ten the next morning. It was cooler and cloudy, so Haley had put the top up on the old Caddy, and rather than shorts, she'd dressed herself in jeans.

Kevin figured she should have been measurably less sexy with denim covering her legs, but she wasn't. He couldn't figure out if it was the cropped T-shirt that barely came to her waist or the confident bounce in her step. He'd noticed it as soon as she'd come out of the bathroom after her shower. She'd greeted him with a smile that had nearly sent him to his knees—fortunately he'd been lying down—and had sashayed across the room.

He tried to tell himself that her curves were no better than average. He'd always been partial to large-breasted women and while Haley didn't have anything to be ashamed of, she didn't qualify as busty. Nor was she as tall as he usually liked. And her—

He stopped himself in mid-thought because he knew he was lying. Big breasts, small breasts, it didn't really matter. Something about Haley got to him. It had almost from the start. It didn't matter if she was covered in burlap and had a tail—he wanted her.

A night of sleep had left his leg slightly less painful and his head clear. Which meant he could remember everything that had happened the previous evening, including Haley's unexpectedly erotic kiss.

The whole thing had been a mistake. He shouldn't have made it clear that while he wouldn't kiss her she was free to kiss him. He should have kept his mouth shut—in more ways than one. Kissing her had taken things to the next level, and it was dangerous up there. After all, who was he kidding? A guy like him and a preacher's daughter? In what universe?

No. The right thing to do was to put the brakes on right now. There wouldn't be any more physical contact. No touching, not kissing. He wouldn't even tease her. They would have impersonal conversations. Maybe about the weather, or the scenery.

Not that there was much to look at right now. They were on the interstate, heading for Wichita. By his calculations they would be there by early afternoon. Haley said they would be lucky to make it by nightfall. She had several stops planned.

"I miss my hair," Haley said.

He turned to look at her. "What?"

She fingered her short blond hair and gave a quick

shrug. "I cut my hair when I left home. It was an impulse. One I'm now regretting."

Regret was good. Haley was determined to take a walk on the wild side and someone needed to teach her consequences.

"Sometimes it's important to think things through," he said.

She nodded.

He knew he shouldn't ask. He really didn't want to know. But he couldn't help himself. "How long was it?"

"To my waist. I mostly wore it back in a braid."

She kept on talking, but he wasn't listening. Instead, he pictured her with long blond hair spilling down her back and over her shoulders. He pictured her naked, on top of him, moving lower, her hair tickling his thighs as she lowered her head and took him in her—

"Kevin?"

"Huh?"

"Are you all right? You seem tense."

He swallowed. "I'm great." And he would be right up until he slid into hell.

"You've mentioned your mother and your brother, but you haven't said anything about your dad. Is he still alive?"

He accepted the change in topic because the alternative was to be tortured by visions of what could never be. As his mind shifted gears, his body stopped heating, although it was going to be a long time until it cooled.

"I don't know where my biological father is," he

said. "I don't know much about him. I know he was a lot older than my mom. She was seventeen when she got pregnant with Nash and me."

Haley sucked in a breath. "That's so young."

"She always says that he was a smooth talker who convinced her they were destined for each other. Before she knew what had happened, she was in his bed. That was in Dallas. He was in town for some kind of convention. After making promises to stay in touch, he went back to whatever rock he'd crawled out from under and she went home. Unfortunately for her, she turned up pregnant."

"He never contacted her again?"

"You got it." There was a time when even thinking about his biological father made Kevin furious, but he'd learned to make peace with that which couldn't be changed. "Unfortunately my mom's parents weren't real supportive. They threw her out the day she turned eighteen. My brother and I were about three months old."

Haley glanced at him, her blue-hazel eyes dark with sympathy. "I don't understand that."

"Neither did she. A friend helped her out. That's when we moved to Possum Landing. For a while, Mom created a fake dead father to help us deal with not having a man around. I guess it was easier for her than answering a lot of questions. When Nash and I were twelve, her folks got in touch with us. They said they wanted to see us. At that point, Mom told us everything that had happened and said it was our decision. She refused to speak with them, but if we wanted a relationship with them, she wasn't going to stand in the way.''

''Your mother sounds like a very special woman.''

''She is. Nash and I talked it over and decided if they hadn't cared about us before, we didn't care about them now.''

''You've never met them?''

''Nope.''

''Any regrets?''

''Not about that.''

''My father is an only child,'' Haley said. ''I have a few aunts and cousins on my mother's side, but they all live in Washington state, so I've never had much to do with them. I always wanted a big family.'' Her voice sounded wistful.

''Then I guess you'll have to grow your own. Have a couple dozen kids.''

''I'd settle for two or three. What about you?''

He shifted slight and adjusted his seat belt. ''I don't know. Maybe.''

''You must have thought about it.''

''Why?''

''Everyone does. It's part of growing up.''

Maybe. ''A couple would be okay, if they weren't like me.''

''You told me some of the stuff you did when you were young and you weren't that bad.''

''Right. Like you would know bad if it came up and bit you on the butt.''

She laughed. ''I probably would recognize it then.''

''I doubt it. Your idea of a walk on the wild side

is being five minutes late for choir practice or having two scoops of ice cream instead of one.''

"So what's yours?"

Seducing an innocent woman like you.

"I did some things I'm not proud of," he said.

"Like what?"

"I stole a car."

"Yeah?" She sounded more impressed than shocked. Figures.

"It wasn't smart. I was arrested and as far as my mom and stepfather were concerned, it was the last straw. They sent me away to military school."

"If you went from being a car thief to being a U.S. Marshal, you must have done something right."

"I didn't like jail and I hated military school. For a couple of months I just felt sorry for myself, but eventually I figured out that I'd earned my place there and if I wanted another chance in the real world, I was going to have to earn that, too."

"Which you did."

"Yeah, but it's not as easy as it sounds. I'm only one mistake from being a screwup again."

She glanced at him. "Being bad sounds like fun."

"No way. Don't go there. There are consequences."

"Everyone always says that."

"Because it's true. Remember your haircut?"

She shook her head. "You have a point there, but maybe it was worth it. Maybe I needed to cut my hair as a symbol of my new life. Besides, just once I would like to be able to do something without worrying about what would happen later."

"Life doesn't work like that. Payback's a bitch."

The clouds had been moving steadily east. The sun broke thorough and Kevin reached for his sunglasses. Haley put hers on, as well.

"You say that so easily."

"Say what?"

"The B-word."

He stared at her. "Bitch?"

She gripped the steering wheel more tightly. "You just swear all the time. You don't even think about it."

"Should I? Are you offended?"

"No. Mostly just curious. I never swear."

"Like that's a surprise."

"I'd like to learn."

He had an instant flash of her saying very bad words, right in his ear. That fact that they were both naked only heightened the appeal of the moment.

"Swearing isn't required," he told her, forcing his mind to something safe like baseball.

"I'd like the option of trying." She glanced at the sky. "Do you mind if I put the top down?"

"No."

She pulled over onto the side of highway and lowered the roof. Kevin pulled on his cap and breathed in the fresh late morning air. Traveling with Haley might take a little longer but he had to admit this was a whole lot better than holing up in some motel waiting until he was well enough to drive.

"I'm thinking of practicing," she said when they were back on the highway. "You know, swearing."

"Go for it."

She looked shocked. "Right now?"

"Why not?"

"What if I get struck by lightning."

"Well, I haven't been struck yet. Although if you're going to do it, I'd start now because the weather report said storms were expected this afternoon."

Her mouth turned up slightly. "Wow. Just like that."

"You don't have to if you don't want to. It's not a big deal."

"It is for me." She sighed. "Why did you kiss me?"

He'd expected a whispered "damn" or "hell." Her question made him shift gears. "You kissed me." Which wasn't the point. He knew what she needed to know.

"Because I wanted to," he admitted.

"But you didn't that first night."

"We've been over this. You were drunk. You didn't know what you were doing."

"And I did last night?"

"At least you were sober. That gave you a fighting chance. You could have said no."

"Did you want to do anything else?" she asked.

He held up both hands. "No way. We're *not* having this conversation."

"Why not?"

"Because I'm not willing to be your first time. I'm not the right guy to have that responsibility."

She didn't say anything. He stared out the front window, knowing that if he looked at her he would see that he'd hurt her feelings. Fine. Better for her to be hurt now than seriously wounded by making love with the wrong man. Haley needed her first time to be after a wedding. Not in some motel with a screwup who knew better.

He leaned forward and flipped on the radio. After spinning the dial, he tuned in a country music station.

"What's it like?"

He almost didn't hear the question. When the words processed, he wished he hadn't. There was no doubt as to what she meant by "it."

"It's okay," he said cautiously, unable to believe they were talking about this.

"Can you be more specific? Is it as great as everyone says?"

He didn't want to be having this conversation. "Don't you have a girlfriend who can explain all this to you?"

"No, and I don't have a mother, either."

Ouch. That one hit below the belt. If he was the best confidant she had, she was in deep trouble.

"Kevin, I'm not trying to make you uncomfortable, I'm just looking for information. I'm too old to be this ignorant. I trust you to tell me the truth. Can we talk about it?"

He sighed. "Fine. We'll talk about it—on the condition that I get to refuse to answer anything that is too weird."

She shot him a grateful grin. "Perfect. So what is it like? Is it amazing?"

"Most of the time. If you care about the person

you're with then sex becomes making love. Otherwise, it's just biology—like a sneeze.''

"I don't understand. What's the difference?''

He wanted to change the subject. He wanted to get out of the car and start walking home, bum leg or not.

"Sex is the act without feelings. Without caring. It's just getting off. Think of a teenage boy desperate to do it with anybody. That's sex. Making love involves more than just the orgasm. It's about connecting.'' He leaned his head back and groaned. "I sound like a guest on 'Oprah.'''

"No. This is great. I understand what you're saying. But what about orgasms? I've read about them, but…well, you know.'' She cleared her throat. "How will I know if I'm having one?''

"If the guy you're with is doing it right, you'll know.''

"That's not very helpful.''

"If you're not sure, it didn't happen. When it does, you won't be wondering.''

At least that was his personal experience with the women of his sexual acquaintance. Not that he was going to say that. Haley would have fifty more questions and he wouldn't want to answer at least forty-nine of them.

As it was, talking about the wild thing was making him think about it. Think about it with *her*—which he wasn't going to do. He stared out at the horizon and tried to disconnect from the conversation. He almost accomplished it, too, right up until her next question.

"What about being naked? Isn't that embarrassing?"

"No. It's fun."

"Not for me. I don't think I could ever be comfortable."

He was being punished. He got that now. His time with Haley was payback for all the stupid things he'd done when he was a kid.

"If you're caught up in the passion and with the right man, you won't mind taking your clothes off. It will feel natural and right. There's nothing more beautiful than a naked woman."

"I don't think so."

He glanced at her and grinned. "That would be a gender difference. For a guy, seeing the woman he's attracted to without her clothes is a peak experience. We want to touch her skin, see how she's put together, explore curves, hollows."

He stopped talking when he realized Haley was gripping the steering wheel just a little too tightly. Speaking of tight, parts of him were getting that way, too. He swore silently.

"Maybe we should talk about something else," he muttered.

Haley surprised him by agreeing.

But after exploring sex—verbally at least—there didn't seem to be much else to say. They drove in silence for nearly half an hour. As they headed toward the middle of Kansas, there were fewer and fewer cars on the road. While there were storm clouds in the distance, the sky overhead was a bright, clear blue.

"Would you mind if I went above the speed

limit?'' Haley asked. ''This car has a lot more power than my old one did. I'd like to see what it can do.''

Kevin figured she would freak out at eighty. ''Go for it,'' he said, and pulled his hat down more securely.

She put her foot on the gas. The big car sped up.

She hit eighty and kept going. Eighty-five, ninety, ninety-five. The wind whipped past them. Haley laughed and he felt his own spirits lighten.

''I didn't think you had it in you,'' he said loudly.

''I want to go a hundred. I've never gone that fast.''

He watched the speedometer hover just below a hundred, then the indicator crossed to one hundred and one, one hundred and two.

''You there. In the yellow Caddy. Pull over right now.''

The loud voice came from above. Haley screamed and instantly lifted her foot from the gas. Kevin glanced up and saw the small plane above them.

''Don't panic,'' he said wryly. ''It wasn't the voice of God. You were caught by the aerial patrol.''

Haley absolutely could not believe this was happening. It seemed so unfair. She'd never gone above the speed limit before in her life. She'd never had a ticket, been in an accident or driven in an unsafe manner. So the very first time she actually cut loose, she got caught.

''Oh, this is bad,'' she whispered as she pulled off to the side of the highway. ''This is so bad.''

''There are always consequences,'' Kevin pointed

out, which didn't make her feel better at all. He should be saying things such as this *wasn't* so bad.

"A spotless record up in flames."

"You're the one who wanted to walk on the wild side."

She glared at him, but he didn't seem intimidated. In fact, she would think he was almost *happy* about her getting caught.

"If I go to prison, you'd better come bail me out," she said.

He actually laughed. "I think the odds of you ending up in the slammer are pretty slim."

She noticed he hadn't actually promised to come rescue her. She covered her face with her hands. What if she did go to prison? She would be forced to call her father and tell him what had happened. He would be so disappointed. Plus he would probably tell Allan and they would come get her together. All her hopes and dreams for a life of her own would end. She would have a record and be trapped back in her old life.

Fifteen minutes later a state patrol car pulled up behind her. She had already dug out her driver's license. She didn't have any official registration for the car, just the paperwork from the car dealer where she'd purchased it.

She watched in her side mirror as the officer got out of his car and walked toward her. She thrust the documents into his hands.

"I'm a worm," she said mournfully. "Really. I'm a horrible person and I know it. Being sorry doesn't help, so I won't even tell you I am. There's no excuse.

Not even a medical emergency. I went fast because I wanted to. I've never had a car with a big engine before and I've never been one who speeds. I mean it's reckless and dangerous, and I'm never like that. I didn't mean to be today, but there was something about the open road and being in a convertible.''

She paused for breath. ''That's not an excuse. In fact it's worse than an excuse. I was immature and selfish. I did make sure there weren't other cars around because I'm not reckless enough to risk other people. I just love my new car so much. Not that it's really new, but it's new to me. But I was wrong. Really wrong. I deserve a ticket.'' She swallowed as tears burned in her eyes. ''You probably want to take me to prison.''

She held up her hands, fingers curled into her palms, wrists next to each other.

The officer slipped off his sunglasses and stared at her. ''You don't actually need me here for this conversation, do you?''

Haley didn't know what to say. She blinked to hold back the tears.

''Wait right here,'' the man said. ''I'm going to run your driver's license through the computer.''

''Oh, I'm not wanted for anything.''

''Uh-huh. You sit tight.''

''Yes, sir.''

Haley slumped back in her seat. She was afraid to close her eyes because she might see her whole life flash by.

Beside her, Kevin sighed. ''A word of advice. Next

time, wait to be charged with something before confessing.''

"No. I was in the wrong. I shouldn't have been speeding.''

"You sure seem anxious to try out prison food.''

She sniffed. "I don't shy away from my responsibilities. As a citizen of this country, I need to abide by the laws of the land.''

The officer returned with her paperwork, her license and an ominous-looking pad.

She tucked her license back into her wallet and handed the paperwork to Kevin to put in the glove box.

"You know you were going over a hundred,'' the man said.

Haley nodded and hung her head. Would they let her make a phone call from jail? Would she have one of those horrible mug shots that made everyone look drawn and guilty?

"What's your story?'' the man asked Kevin, pointing to the bandage on his leg.

"Work-related injury,'' Kevin said.

"He was shot,'' Haley offered, which earned her a disgusted look from Kevin.

"What?'' she asked, confused by his reaction. "It's what happened.''

"You have some ID?'' the officer asked.

Kevin nodded and pulled out his wallet. He flipped it to an official-looking document and passed it to Haley who handed it out the open window.

"U.S. Marshal?'' the man asked.

Kevin nodded. "I got caught up in the prison riot.''

"He'd been delivering a prisoner," Haley offered helpfully. "When there was trouble, they paged him to come back. He was hit in the head and shot which is why I'm driving him home. He's not allowed to fly."

"Your wife?" the man asked, pointing at Haley.

Haley felt herself blushing.

Kevin sighed heavily. "No. Just a friend."

"A friend with a lead foot." The officer handed Kevin back his ID, then turned to Haley. "Keep it at the speed limit, miss."

She blinked at him. "What?"

"I'm letting you off with a warning. If this happens again, I'm hauling you in for reckless driving. You understand?"

He was letting her go? For real? She couldn't believe it.

"I—sure. Yes, I understand. The speed limit. I can do that."

"Have a nice day."

The man flipped his pad closed and returned to his patrol car. Haley sat there until he'd pulled out onto the highway. Then she leaned her head back, raised her arms and yelled out a big "Thank you" to the universe.

"I didn't get a ticket," she told Kevin.

He didn't seem as excited. "I know."

"Isn't it amazing."

"You were lucky. He felt bad because I was shot." His gaze narrowed. "You *deserved* a ticket."

She refused to be anything but thrilled by the change in circumstances.

"I'm not going to prison. I don't have to call my father or—" She hesitated. "Or anyone else. No one is going to know. Isn't this wonderful?"

"No, it's not. You need to learn a lesson in consequences."

As she started her engine, a delightful thought occurred to her. "Maybe there aren't any. Maybe that's just a line made up by worried parents."

Kevin groaned. "Why did I know you were going to say that?"

She checked her mirror, then pulled back onto the highway. "Isn't this the best day? Aren't we having a wonderful time? Isn't life terrific?"

Kevin leaned back and closed his eyes. "You're giving me a headache."

"You need to lighten up."

"What I need is a drink."

Chapter Seven

Shortly after four that afternoon, they stopped at a seamy antique store outside of Wichita. Kevin watched as Haley pounced on various "treasures." Her squeals of delight brightened the eyes of the owner, as the sixty-something woman calculated profits. Kevin didn't have the heart to warn her that Haley's idea of a magical find didn't match most people's and was rarely over three dollars.

In almost seven hours he and his traveling companion had barely gone two hundred miles. It turned out that Haley not only had a burning desire to explore every shop, out-of-the-way museum and monument within twenty miles of the highway, she had the attention span of a gnat once they got there. She bounced from exhibit to exhibit, item to item, barely pausing long enough to see anything, which made him question why she'd wanted to stop in the first place. She also had a bladder the size of a thimble and yet insisted on drinking quart-size bottles of water, which meant there were pit stops every twenty or thirty miles.

She should have been making him crazy—instead, he found himself completely charmed. Shortly after lunch—where they'd stopped at Mom's Café and Home Cooking Emporium—he'd realized that with Haley, it was all about the journey. After being cooped up for years in a small town and never going anywhere, she wanted the adventure of exploring life. And if that meant examining a stuffed armadillo, then that's what she did.

"Kevin, look!"

He followed the sound of her voice and found her crouched over a bucket of arrowheads. She held two in her hand and was digging through the rest, apparently looking for a matched set.

"Aren't they cool?" she asked, holding out her finds to him.

"They're great."

Arrowheads? She was so happy to have found them that he didn't have the heart to point out they were so plentiful that she could practically pick them up on the side of the road.

"How many are you looking for?" he asked, thinking that if it was too many, he should plan on them spending the night here.

"Three. And they have to be exactly the same. What about this one?"

She handed him an arrowhead. He compared it

with the others and reluctantly gave it back. "Too round. You want one that's more pointy."

"Okay."

She happily dug away, finally producing the triplet to the two she'd already chosen. When she stood, she offered one of those generous, beaming smiles that always made him think that the men in her hometown were idiots for not snapping her up the second she turned eighteen.

"Let's go inside," she said, pointing to the rickety building that could almost pass for a store.

Kevin leaned on his cane and mentally braced himself for more stuffed dead animals and maybe some old clothes. She seemed real fond of them, although she'd yet to buy either.

Heavy clouds had obscured the sun, so it was dark inside. Haley walked down crooked rows, pausing to admire an old cookie jar and a set of mismatched spoons. When she reached the back, she called his name.

"It's Depression glass," she said when he joined her in front of an old glass case. "My mom used to collect it. We have it back at the house. My father always told me it was mine when I married."

She pressed her fingers against the case. Her full mouth pulled into a straight line and her eyes turned sad.

Kevin didn't know if she was missing her mother, her father, her old life or just the promise of whatever future she'd run away from. He'd been putting bits and pieces of the puzzle of her life together since he'd met her and decided to take one of his theories for a test drive.

"You didn't want it enough to get married?" he asked.

She looked at him and rolled her eyes. "No one gets married to inherit a collection."

"Depends on what's in it. I could be had for the right price."

She laughed. "You are so lying. Aren't you the man who explained the difference between having sex and making love? Men who make love cannot be bought."

"You're wrong. I like to think of myself as a potential gigolo."

"Really?"

He'd dug the pit himself, then had pretty much fallen into it all on his own. He took a single step back. "Ah, no. Not really."

She was still chuckling as she headed up the next aisle. An old tintype caught her attention. It showed several lawmen standing next to their horses.

"Your ancestors," she said, holding it out to him. "They were good guys, just like you."

He knew he couldn't describe himself that way, but it wasn't for lacking of trying. He put the picture back on the shelf.

"I'd like to get to Texas before Christmas," he said, pushing lightly on the small of her back. "Unless you see another armadillo that tempts you, I suggest we pay for your treasures and hit the road."

"You're so pushy."

"And you could happily shop in a used sock store."

She shook her head and walked to the counter where she paid for her three arrowheads. "You underestimate the value of treasure," she told him.

"No, I don't share your definition of the word."

"These are a part of our country's heritage."

Haley collected her change and thanked the woman, then headed toward her car. Kevin didn't understand that little things like arrowheads and the glass vase she'd purchased after lunch were all symbols. Sure, a lot of people would think they were junk, but to her they were the talismans of her journey to freedom. She tucked the arrowheads into a small paper bag with an old leather bookmark.

Kevin came up beside her. "I'll call them treasures as long as I don't have to claim any of them."

"Fair enough."

He jerked his head toward the back seat. "What's your dad going to say when he sees all that? Will it fit in with the family decor?"

"I'm not going to be living with him anymore. I'm going to get my own place."

Haley spoke the words with more bravado than she felt. When she was done, she hunched her shoulders, half expecting lightning to strike her. But nothing happened.

She straightened and glanced at the gathering clouds. Was it possible that moving out on her own wasn't as completely horrible and selfish as she'd first thought?

She almost asked Kevin, but she knew he wouldn't

understand the question. For him, life was simple. He was a man who knew what he wanted and either went after it or did it. He didn't fret about other people's opinions or expectations. He wasn't afraid of anything. If only she could be more like that.

"So where are you moving to?" he asked as he opened the passenger door and slid onto the seat.

"I don't know. Once I know where I'm working, I'll find a place close by. It doesn't have to be big or anything." As long as it was hers and no one else's.

"Do you have any specific places in mind?"

"No. I want to teach, and I can do that anywhere. It's what I've wanted since I was a little girl."

"What do you teach?"

She sat next to him and smiled. "Middle school math."

"You're kidding?" He looked her over. "If my middle school math teacher had looked like you I would have been a whole lot more interested in algebra."

His compliment pleased her. Kevin had made it clear that he was attracted to her, at least a little. She still thought he was good-looking and very sexy, but the more they were together, the more she liked who he was.

A rumbling in the distance caught her attention. She turned toward the horizon and studied the dark clouds. "That looks like a bad storm."

Kevin nodded. "I hate to say this, but we should probably find a place for the night."

"Okay."

She spoke casually, but her heart was pounding

hard. They were going to have another night together. Last night they'd kissed. Would they again tonight? Would they do more?

She started the engine, then put up the convertible top. As they drove down the narrow road that led back to the highway, the first drops of rain hit the windshield.

"Let's look for a place close to a decent restaurant," he said. "I'm up to going out for dinner. What about you?"

She thought of the pretty summer dresses she'd bought. This would be her first chance to wear one. "That sounds like fun."

He shifted in his seat and stretched out his leg.

"Do you want another pain pill?" she asked.

"I'll wait until bedtime. If we talk it will distract me. I'll even let you go first. Why do you have to run away to become a teacher?"

The question shouldn't have surprised her, but it still made her tense. She tightened her hold on the steering wheel and tried to figure out how much to tell him.

"I don't know how to explain my life without sounding like a spineless idiot," she admitted.

"I don't think you're either."

She gave him a quick smile, then turned her attention back to the road. The highway was up ahead. She put on her blinker, then merged with the traffic.

"You're nice to say that, but running away, as you put it, has shown me that I've been both for a long time. I guess it became a habit. I remember being a little girl. Nice ladies from the congregation would come over and help me pick out clothes for church. They would brush my hair and put ribbons at the end of my braid. They always told me that I had to be a good girl and make my daddy proud. They said that I was the minister's daughter and that meant I was held to a higher standard. For a long time I thought that meant I had to be tall.''

Kevin didn't laugh. ''That's a lot for a kid to have to deal with.''

''Some of it wasn't so bad. I liked that someone was always around to help with homework or take me shopping. But they never stayed. Eventually they went home to their own families, their own children, and I was left alone with my dad.''

''He never remarried, right?''

She shook her head. ''A lot of people said that he would, but he never even dated. I hoped he would. I wanted a mother of my own. I wanted to feel that I belonged. To someone. To a family. But that never happened. And then I grew up and I stopped waiting to belong.''

''I don't believe that.''

She didn't look at him—she didn't dare. Was Kevin right? Did she still want to be a part of something? She supposed that everyone did in one way or the other.

''Maybe you're right,'' she admitted. ''I found myself not wanting to disappoint anyone. Doing what was expected wasn't all that hard, so I did it. I made the right choices.''

''Which meant not moving away?''

''Yeah.'' She sighed. ''I don't want you to think

my father was a difficult man, because he wasn't. He's wonderful. So loving and giving. We're all lucky to have him.''

"You and the congregation?"

"Right. He never punished me or yelled at me, but I knew when he was unhappy with me. I could see it in his eyes. So I did what I was told. Like the summer I turned eleven and the ladies in the church didn't think I should be running around in shorts anymore. So I wore dresses. And when I went to high school, three different women talked to me about the perils of having a bad reputation and how easy it was to take the wrong road. So I was always careful never to do that.''

"In the end you worried so much, you didn't date at all."

She nodded. The rain came down a little heavier and she turned on the windshield wipers.

"My father always hoped I'd marry a minister. I wanted to study to be a teacher, but everyone knows that ministers' wives have to play the piano, so I studied music instead.''

"I thought you said you had your teaching credentials."

"I do." She shrugged. "It was a small act of rebellion, but when I went back to college and got my master's of fine arts in music, I completed the rest of the courses I need for my teaching certificate.''

"A quiet rebellion?"

"One I never confessed to." She bit her lower lip. "I'm not very proud of that. I should have told my father the truth.''

"Maybe he shouldn't have put you in the position of having to hide your heart's desire."

She'd never thought of it that way. Could her father have made things easier for her?

"We're about as different as it's possible to be," Kevin told her. "When I was growing up I never met a rule I didn't want to break."

"Sounds like fun. I would have liked that, but breaking the rules is more difficult, coming to it this late in life."

"You're making progress. Look at your car."

"Good point." Her father would never have approved of the car. Allan would have gone one step further and forced her to return it.

"What about that place?"

Kevin pointed across the highway to a small motel sharing a parking lot with a steak house. It was still early but there were several cars parked outside the restaurant. Always a good sign.

"Works for me," she said. "I'll take the next off-ramp and circle back."

When she pulled in front of the motel, the rain seemed to let up a little. They climbed out and started toward the front office. Kevin was limping pretty badly.

"Does it hurt?" she asked as she walked next to him.

"I'm stiff from sitting so long. I just need to stretch my muscles out."

She eyed his drawn features and the tightness around his mouth. She would guess he needed another dose of pain medicine, but he was being stubborn about taking as many as he was allowed.

"Suffering isn't macho," she muttered.

He grinned. "Sure it is. You're fussing over me. If nothing hurt, you wouldn't give me the time of day."

They both knew that wasn't true, but she liked his teasing her, so she didn't say anything.

They approached the front desk, where an old man gave them a toothy grin. "What can I get you folks?"

Haley's mind hiccuped. What did they need? One room? Last night she hadn't thought twice about sharing quarters with him. He'd been injured and completely out of it. But tonight was different. He was certainly alert. Plus, they'd spent a whole day together, which somehow made sharing a room more intimate than it had been the previous evening. Yet he was still hurt and what if he needed her help? She didn't want to be too far away. Was she being overly cautious about something that didn't really matter?

Before she could find the answer to any of her questions, Kevin spoke. "We'd like adjoining rooms, please."

"Sure thing."

The old man collected two keys, then handed them each a registration card. As Haley filled hers out, she tried to figure out if she was relieved or disappointed. Probably a bit of both. While she'd *wanted* to stay in the same room as Kevin, she was also terrified to do so.

"How's the steak place next door?" Kevin asked as he handed over his completed card.

"Best steaks in three counties," the manager said.

"I suggest you go early. The wait'll be shorter and we're expectin' some pretty bad storms tonight. Might even have a twister come on through."

"Beats cable," Kevin said. "You finished?"

Haley nodded and gave the man her card. He took an imprint of Kevin's credit card, accepted her cash, then gave them each a key.

"Ground floor at the end. Should be plenty quiet. Enjoy your stay."

"Thanks."

Kevin headed for the door. Haley trailed after him.

"Was he saying we could have a tornado tonight?"

"Looks that way."

Except for *The Wizard of Oz,* she'd never had any personal experience with that kind of storm.

"What do we do?" she asked.

He glanced at her. "We go have a steak dinner."

"I meant about the storm."

"There's nothing *to* do. If one comes through, it comes through."

"But where do we go? Is there a storm cellar or something? What about my car?"

He put an arm around her. "For a minister's daughter, you don't have very much faith."

"I have plenty of faith. What I don't have is an escape plan if a tornado comes."

"If we hear the sirens, we'll get in the bathtub and pull a mattress over ourselves."

Did people really do that sort of thing? "It doesn't sound very comfortable."

"It beats getting hit on the head by a dresser."

They got back into her car and she drove down to

the end of the building. After collecting their luggage, they each went into their own rooms.

Haley stood in the middle of a bedroom that looked a lot like the other motel rooms she'd stayed in over the past few days. But instead of flipping on the television to check out the cable channels, she stared at the closed and locked door separating her room from Kevin's.

Should she open it? Were they semi-sharing quarters? If they weren't going to open it, why had he asked for adjoining rooms? And why was her stomach getting all tight and knotted from thinking about this?

She was rescued by a knock on the door. Haley unfastened the bolt and pulled it open. Kevin smiled.

"Want to keep these open?" he asked.

"Sure."

He stepped into her room. "Have you noticed these places all look the same?"

"Pretty much. I hope the cable's good."

"So you can shop on that home shopping program you like so much?"

"I haven't actually bought anything yet."

"Give it time." He glanced at his watch. "When do you want to go to dinner?"

"I'm hungry now."

"Me, too."

Haley glanced down at her jeans. "I'd like to get changed."

His gaze narrowed. "You're not putting on shorts, are you?"

"To go to a restaurant?" She was shocked. "I'll wear a dress."

"Uh-huh. Is that going to be better or worse for me?"

"I don't understand the question."

Kevin sighed. "I know. See you in twenty minutes."

He retreated to his room, half closing his adjoining door, but leaving hers open.

She hesitated, wondering what on earth he'd meant, then she realized she didn't have much time and hurried toward the suitcase she'd brought in. After collecting a dress and the small bag of cosmetics she'd purchased at Wal-Mart, she ducked into the bathroom.

Haley washed her face and applied moisturizer, then studied the contents of her makeup bag. The basics were easy. She'd applied mascara a few times and lip gloss was self-explanatory, but what about eye shadow and base?

She shook the flesh-colored bottle, but chickened out at the thought of putting that goopy liquid all over her face. There was a little diagram on the back of the eye shadow compact, showing where each of the three colors should go. She followed the instructions, using a minimal amount of color, then smudging everything with her finger.

Huh. Maybe it was just the light in here, but she thought her eyes looked bigger and more blue. Was it possible that shading her eyelids had really worked?

Mascara went on next, then lip gloss. She studied her hair, but there wasn't much she could do with the short, flyaway style. Unfortunately.

Next was her outfit for the evening. She pulled off

her jeans and T-shirt and stood in her underwear while she studied her choice. The breezy summer dress she'd bought had skinny straps. Very skinny straps. Straps that were much, much skinnier than her bra straps. She hadn't noticed that before.

Okay, so what exactly did she do about that? She didn't want her bra showing, but the alternative was unthinkable. She would be punished for sure. After all, wearing shorts was one thing, but going without a bra? A tornado would suck her up in a heartbeat.

Still, showing her bra straps was just plain tacky. A lot of people seemed to do it, but to her it was like going out with her slip hanging two inches below her dress. Yuck. Which meant she could either pick another dress, wear this one with a bra or wear it without and risk potentially cosmic consequences.

Haley squeezed her eyes tightly shut and turned away from the mirror. Without even daring to breathe, she undid her bra and let it fall to the floor. Then she pulled the dress over her head and tugged it into place. Only then did she dare to open her eyes and face her reflection.

The first thing she noticed was the big old tag hanging down nearly to her waist. She pulled that off, then held out her arms to try to see if anyone could really tell she wasn't wearing a bra. It wasn't as if her chest was huge; if she didn't move too much, neither did her breasts. The fabric was lined, so nothing physically showed through. Still, Haley felt more than a little naked.

Reminding herself that she was supposed to be living life on the wild side now, and determined to ignore the sensation of being unclothed, she went in search of her strappy sandals. She'd barely finished fastening them when Kevin knocked on the adjoining door.

"Are you ready?" he asked.

"Um, I think so."

She stood and grabbed for her purse as he walked into her room.

"I'm looking forward to having a steak tonight," he said. "There's nothing like a bullet wound to make a man want red—"

He came to a stop about three steps into her room. His mouth stayed open, but he wasn't talking. His gaze moved over her, starting at the top of her head and slowly moving down to her bare toes, then making the return trip. She couldn't tell if he'd hesitated on her chest or not and she didn't really want to know. Instead, she stared slightly over his left shoulder and waited for him to say something. Anything.

"You look amazing."

She blinked, then smiled at him. "Really?"

"Absolutely. Apparently preachers' daughters from Ohio clean up real good."

His compliment made her beam. "You don't think it's too much? I mean I was worried that the dress was a little too…" She shrugged. "Racy."

She wasn't sure but she thought he might have swallowed.

"It's perfect. I'm going to be fighting guys off all evening. Maybe I should bring my gun."

She knew he was teasing, but his words still made her feel good. No one had ever even hinted that she might be attractive enough to capture the attention of more than one man at a time.

She studied his new jeans pulled on over his bandage and the tucked-in polo shirt that revealed his broad chest and narrow waist. "You look nice, too."

"Thanks. Let's go eat. I'm starved."

They made their way out of the motel room and across the parking lot to the restaurant. The hostess showed them to a booth right away. Haley slid in across from Kevin. He settled himself in place and hooked his cane over the edge of the table. She picked up the menu the hostess had left, but instead of opening it, she studied the restaurant.

Booths lined the walls of the open room. There were votive candles on the tables and sawdust swirls on the floor. A bar filled the left side of the building and she could just catch the faint sound of a country music song.

This was the kind of place people came to have fun and Haley found herself wanting to join in. Her foot tapped in time with the music and she couldn't help smiling as she turned her attention back to Kevin.

"This is great," she said.

"Your kind of place?"

She'd never thought of herself as having a "place." A type of establishment that appealed to her. She'd never been the one making the decisions about where to go to eat at a restaurant. But if it were up to her...

She nodded. "Absolutely. What about you?"

"Show me a good steak and I'm a happy man."

"Hi, there. Can I get you a drink?"

Haley turned her attention to the woman standing by their table. She was tall, busty and blond. Her low-cut spandex top clung to curves impressive enough to make a rock star look twice. Haley suddenly felt as if she were playing dress-up and not doing a very good job of things.

Kevin shrugged. "I'm off liquor because of the painkillers. What would you like?"

Haley couldn't think that fast. She didn't know the names of drinks and she didn't want to appear stupid in front of the centerfold-material blonde. She was about to ask the woman to give her a minute when Kevin came to her rescue.

"Maybe you'd allow me to pick a glass of wine for you," he said.

"I'd like that."

He glanced at the wine list on the back of the menu. "The lady will have a glass of Pinot Noir."

The waitress scribbled the order, flashed a smile and left. Haley was too caught up in the words "the lady will have" to much notice. She knew it was just good manners and all that, but no one had ever called her a lady before. Not like that. She'd been instructed to *act* like a lady for most of her life, which wasn't the same thing at all.

A young man brought them water and bread, then their waiter took their order. She and Kevin both picked steaks, although she chose a petite fillet and he went for the large New York cut. Seconds later, her wine appeared.

She eyed the purplish-red wine. If she hadn't liked

community hobby. Everyone had a piece of my life but me.''

She rested her fingertips on the base of her wineglass. "I've already explained that I didn't date much in high school or college. I really wanted to find someone, though. I'd always imagined myself as a wife and a mother. I love kids.''

"Then you picked the right profession.''

She brightened at the thought. "Yes, I did. I think I would be a very good teacher. Not that anyone else agreed with me.''

"What about the guy?''

"I met Allan the summer I turned twenty. I was home from college and he'd just been hired as the associate pastor. He's a few years older than me.''

Kevin didn't say anything. He just watched her with his dark eyes and kept his expression unreadable. She would guess that none of this made sense to him. Kevin had never let anyone run his life. He'd been in charge of his own destiny for years. Why couldn't she be more like that?

"So you were instantly attracted to him?'' he asked.

"No. Not really. I mean, he was nice and everything, but I didn't even see him as a guy until my father's secretary said something about him being good-looking. Then someone else mentioned he was single and a third person told me he'd said he thought I was pretty. After a while I got the message that the congregation thought it would be wonderful if we started dating, so we did.''

"How did Allan feel about the decision being made for him?"

"I don't know. At the time I would have said it was his idea, too, but now..." She sighed. "I'm not sure."

"So you dated?"

"Yeah. He was fun and interesting, but he had some really specific ideas about the woman in his life. He didn't want me wearing jeans, not even at home. I think if I'd put on shorts, he would have had a heart attack. When I told him about wanting to be a teacher, he talked about how beautifully I played the piano, and how important that was for a preacher's wife. He encouraged me to volunteer, to not have any friends of my own or any opinions."

She took a sip of her wine. "I didn't get that all at once. Over the past few years I've figured out that his 'suggestions' were really instructions. I'd never felt in control of my life and suddenly I had less control than before. I was sneaking around at college, secretly taking courses for my teaching credentials while getting a masters in music."

"So why did you stay with him?"

"Because it was expected. Because I didn't know what love was and everyone told me I was in love with him. After a while, I thought I was. So when he proposed, I said yes."

She waited for a reaction, but except for the faint twitch of a muscle in his jaw, Kevin didn't react.

"Did you marry him?" he asked.

Her eyes widened. "No! I wouldn't be here with you if I was married. I wouldn't have...have..." If there was a time to swear, this was it. She could feel her face getting hot.

She glanced around to make sure no one was paying attention to them, then leaned forward and lowered her voice. "I would never have kissed you if I'd been married."

"Fair enough. So what happened to the engagement?"

"We were supposed to be married at the end of the month."

Finally Kevin looked surprised. "This month."

"Uh-huh. Things hadn't been going well between us, but the wedding plans were a runaway train and I didn't know how to stop them. Everyone was involved. Over three hundred invitations went out." She briefly closed her eyes against the memory of addressing all those envelopes. It had taken her weeks. She'd wanted to ask for help, but Allan had believed it was the bride's responsibility to do it herself, that it showed respect for the guests.

"I couldn't talk to anyone and even if I could, what could I have complained about? That Allan didn't listen? That sometimes I felt I wasn't a person to him?" She shook her head. "They would have said I was ungrateful."

"How didn't he listen?"

"Oh, in different ways. I wanted kids right away but he didn't, so three months ago he made an appointment and took me to my doctor to get me on the Pill. I wanted to go to Hawaii for our honeymoon, but he wanted to go to Branson, so that's where we were going. Silly stuff."

Kevin reached across the table and put his hand on top of hers. His dark gaze seemed to see down to the depths of her being.

"None of that is silly," he said quietly. "Marriage is supposed to be a partnership, not a dictatorship. Allan was wrong not to pay attention to what would make you happy."

No one had ever said that to her before. A lightness filled Haley and made her want to float up to the ceiling like an escaped balloon.

"Yeah?"

He nodded. "The guy sounds like a jerk. So what happened? You finally couldn't stand it anymore and took off?"

Suddenly ashamed, she withdrew her hand and ducked her head. "No," she whispered. "I didn't have the backbone for that. I was having a lot of second thoughts, but I was afraid to say anything. Then Allan came to me and told me he wasn't sure he was in love with me. He wanted to postpone the wedding."

Kevin muttered something that sounded like a string of really bad words. She tried not to listen.

"I got mad," she admitted, looking at him again. "I wasn't hurt, I was furious. I couldn't believe that I'd given up my entire life and everything I wanted for a man who wasn't even sure he was in love with me."

"So you ran."

"I escaped," she corrected. "Right then and there I vowed I would never again, as long as I lived, do what other people thought was right. I would only do what *I* thought was right for me. So I left home and started driving to Hawaii.'' She thought about the beautiful pictures she'd seen over the years. ''I've always wanted to visit the islands.''

Kevin watched Haley's expression turn wistful. His gut twisted in a rage he hadn't felt in years. He wanted to go find the jerk who'd treated her so badly and pound his self-centered, egotistic self into dust. He didn't have time for bullies and that's just what Allan had been. He sensed right away that the guy was stronger than Haley so he'd assumed that had given him the right to run her life and dictate terms.

Somewhere along the way Allan had decided it was all right for him to be in charge, to know best.

''I'm impressed you managed to get your teaching degree, despite everything,'' he said.

''I can be patient.'' A smile curved up the corners of her mouth. ''And maybe a little bit sneaky. Honestly, I hated lying to everyone but getting that degree was really important to me and I didn't think it was such a horrible thing. It's not like I wanted to be a stripper. Besides, we need more teachers.''

The waitress appeared with their salads. Haley reached for the bread basket and offered it to him. When he'd taken a roll, she picked one for herself.

''You're better off without Allan,'' he said. ''Do you believe that?''

She nodded, then paused and shook her head. ''I tell myself that. I want to believe it, and most of the time I do. I just wish I didn't feel so guilty. It's complicated.''

''Life often is.''

"Mine wasn't before." She took a sip of the wine. "I really like this. You made a great choice."

He grinned. "Stick with me, kid, and I'll show you the good life."

As soon as the words were out of his mouth he wanted to call them back. Haley's face brightened and she beamed at him. He felt both ten feet tall and as small as the biggest lowlife on the planet. While he knew she was perfectly safe in his company, he also knew how much he wanted her. Liking her was fine— Haley was a likable sort of person. But sex?

He'd reformed his ways, become one of the good guys. He had a bad feeling that giving in to Haley's particular brand of temptation was a slick, steep road back to hell.

"Let me rephrase that," he said. "I'm not someone to stick with."

"Of course you are. You're one of the best people I've ever met."

"Not even by half. My mother used to drag me to church every week, but it sure as hell didn't take. I stopped going as soon as I could."

"What does church have to do with anything?" She speared several lettuce pieces but didn't eat. "Allan and I used to argue about that all the time. I've always believed that God is so much more than a building. People find Him wherever they need Him. But for Allan, church was everything.

"I'll agree that belonging to a church provides a sense of community and structure. A good pastor or rabbi or whatever can encourage people and teach them to be their best selves, but God is the point. Do you believe in God?''

He'd been so caught up in her words, in her beliefs, which were a bit of a surprise, that he almost didn't catch the question.

''Yes,'' he answered without thinking.

She shrugged. ''So if you believe, then how can you keep from worshiping and giving thanks, in whatever form that takes? Appreciating the beauty of a morning, or being grateful for being alive. Isn't that praise?''

''I've never thought of it like that,'' he admitted.

''I think about it a lot. Like I said, Allan didn't agree with me. For him if someone didn't belong to the church, they weren't of value. Sometimes I was afraid that for him it was all about how things looked, not how they were inside.''

He shook his head. ''You were wrong before when you said you didn't have any backbone. You're pure steel. I admire that.''

Her eyes lit up. ''Really?''

''Allan was an idiot for not seeing it.'' He tore open his roll. ''So did you love him?''

He asked the question for a couple of reasons. First, because he needed to change the subject. His compliments had a way of making her see him as something of a prize. For another, as much as he didn't want to know the answer, he figured that if she was still in love with the guy, the information would be enough to crank down his desire to escort Haley right into his bed. He might be a bit of a bastard, but he didn't poach.

"I don't know," she admitted. "I thought I did, but now things are all muddled. Maybe I don't know what romantic love is. What about you? Have you been in love?"

"Once. A long time ago."

"Did you marry her?"

"She was already married. I didn't know. I was looking for forever and she just wanted a good time."

"I'm sorry."

"Hey, it happens." He could tell the story now without feeling the pain, but when it had happened... He didn't want to think about that. "I got over it. Maybe I wasn't as in love as I thought."

"I want to be swept away," she said. "I want love to crash over me like a wave and carry me out into the ocean."

"Sounds dangerous."

"It sounds exciting."

He looked at her and their eyes locked. Kevin felt a rushing sensation deep in his chest. He didn't know what it was and he didn't want to know. He could smell the danger all around. But he wouldn't go there. Not with Haley. She wasn't for him. He'd known that from the beginning. But that didn't mean he had to like it.

Kevin knew he was being punished. Or tested. Or maybe both. He probably deserved the former and was going to fail the latter, which was interesting but not particularly helpful in his current situation.

He was in pain. He told himself that over and over again, as if it would make a damn bit of difference.

Nothing about the situation was sexy or erotic. He rubbed his hand over his face and figured there was no point in lying to himself. Once Haley was in the room, everything became sexually charged—at least for him. Sitting on the bed in nothing but his shirt and briefs while she changed his bandage was about the most *physically* interesting thing to happen to him in months. Maybe years.

Damn depressing, he thought, leaning his head back on the pillow he'd propped up against the headboard and tried to concentrate on the game on TV. He'd ended a relationship going nowhere about four months ago. He and Millie had been on-and-off lovers for nearly six months. What did it say about his life when having a bandage changed on his gunshot leg was sexier than having sex with someone else?

He heard a soft sound and opened his eyes. Haley had walked into his bedroom, her hands filled with tubes, bandages and tape. She dropped her supplies next to him and settled on the edge of the bed.

"How does it feel?" she asked.

Hard.

He clenched his teeth and tried to think about carburetor parts, but it didn't help. Just knowing she was wearing that damn dress without a bra killed him. He didn't even have to look at her breasts, either. He was hard and getting harder by the heartbeat.

"Kevin?"

He stared at her. "I'm fine," he muttered.

"Are you sure? You look kind of…" Her voice trailed off. "Uncomfortable."

Good a word as any, he thought with a laugh. "I'm okay. Just change the bandage."

He stared at the ceiling as she messed with her supplies and reached for the scissors, then knew the exact moment she'd caught sight of his "problem." Her breath caught and he felt her gaze shift to his face.

"Ignore it," he said, still looking upward and wondering what he'd done to deserve this in his life.

She didn't speak, didn't move. As far as he could tell, she wasn't even breathing. Finally he looked at her.

Her eyes were the size of baseballs, her mouth was parted and color stained her cheeks.

"It doesn't mean anything," he told her. "I'm a man, you're a woman. I find you attractive and we're alone in a bedroom. It happens."

She swallowed. "I've never seen a man before—you know. That."

The "that" in question pulsed slightly.

"C-can I ask you some questions?"

He would rather she hacked off his arm. He sighed. "Sure. What do you want to know?"

More color flooded her face. "So you're, um, aroused?"

"Isn't that obvious?"

She turned away. "Not to me."

Damn. He'd inadvertently sucker punched her, which only proved he was the wrong guy for the job. Knowing he was courting twenty-seven kinds of trouble, he touched her arm.

"Sorry, Haley. I'm not handling this well. I'm a

little uncomfortable with the situation. At thirty-one I should be able to control myself better. Go ahead and ask your questions.''

He was talking about his erection, but he didn't know if she would understand that. Either way, she seemed to accept his apology. She turned her attention back to his face.

She bit her lower lip. He watched as curiosity battled with modesty. Curiosity won.

''I've heard that blood fills, um, it and it gets bigger. Does that hurt? I'm asking because I broke my arm once and it really swelled up and it hurt more than anything.''

Despite the strange situation, he couldn't help laughing. ''No, it doesn't feel like a broken arm. There's tension and an aching when I get hard, but no physical pain. Blood flows in and eventually flows out.''

She glanced down at his lap, then back at his face. ''I thought it would stick out more.''

He held in a grin. ''It does. If I were to take off my underwear, it would stick straight out.''

Her expression turned intrigued.

''No way,'' he said before she could ask. ''That's not going to happen. Looking would lead to other things and I'm not into defiling virgins.''

''You'd probably be very good at it.''

''We're not going to find out.''

She sighed heavily. ''And you say you're not a good guy. Someone bad would have already taken advantage of me.''

A good guy wouldn't want her so much, he

thought, but didn't share that with her. Instead, he shifted his leg.

"Go ahead and torture me," he said. "I'll watch the Braves kick butt."

He focused on the third inning, then groaned when the team left two men on. Haley worked efficiently, peeling off the old bandage, applying the ointment and putting on the new dressing. He'd only had one pain pill that morning and wouldn't take another until bedtime. He was already improving, which was a good thing. He had a feeling he was going to need all his strength to resist Haley.

When she finished, she stood and carried her supplies back into her room. He relaxed. At least that hurdle had been passed. Maybe tomorrow he should change his own bandage. It would be a whole lot easier if he—

She reappeared in the doorway. "Would you want me if I wasn't a virgin?"

Had he been standing the question would have knocked him on his ass. There were a thousand safe ways to answer that question. A thousand games he could play with her. Instead, he stared into her eyes and knew he could only tell her the truth. After the hell that bastard Allan had put her through, she deserved that.

"I want you now. The difference is, if you weren't a virgin, I'd act on it."

He'd hoped that would send her running, but Haley being Haley crossed to the bed and sat next to him. Before he could gather his defenses, she leaned forward and kissed him.

In seconds he was drowning in her softness, in the taste of her and the quick, eager strokes of her hot tongue. She was innocent, tempting and a damn fine kisser all in one package. Was it his fault that his arms came around her and he pulled her close? He was a man, not a statue.

He was used to lush women with curves to spare. Haley was slight in his arms, but still appealing. He angled his head so he could kiss her more deeply, following her back into her mouth, tracing the sweetness of the inside of her lower lip, then circling her tongue with his. He tasted her, teased her, stroked her. They established a dance that sent fire to points south. Hard became harder and the ache made the pain in his leg feel like a mosquito bite.

He cupped her face, his fingers stroking her soft skin. She smelled like flowers and candy. She tasted like heaven. When her hands settled on his shoulders, he wanted to pull free and rip off his shirt. He wanted her hands on his chest, his back, his groin. He wanted her to rub him until he exploded. No, he wanted to bury himself inside her and then explode.

Haley nearly lost her breath when Kevin bit down on her lower lip. He nibbled her there, then soothed the sensitive skin with a quick lick. From there he moved to her jaw, biting, kissing, making her feel things she'd never felt before. The world was spinning and she was caught up in the vortex, tossed first one way, then the other. She couldn't think. She didn't want it ever to stop.

But while her brain wasn't working, her body

seemed to be doing just great. Every touch, every point of contact, was exquisite pleasure. Yes, of course Allan had kissed her, but it hadn't been with this fire or passion. She'd never felt a trembling in her chest before. Her breasts had never seem too tight and uncomfortable for her clothes. She wasn't even wearing a bra and yet she felt confined. Between her legs little jolts of heavy, throbbing electricity made her press her knees together as if to hold in something she couldn't really contain.

Kevin kissed his way down her neck. He shifted and reached for the strap on her dress, then pushed it off her shoulder. When his mouth settled just over her collar bone, she caught her breath. How could that be such a sensitive place on her body? Was he as sensitive?

Caught up in the feel of his mouth and lips and tongue, she had trouble forcing herself to move but eventually she slid her hands down to the front of his chest. His muscles moved, tightening and released as she slid over them. His body was so different from hers. Angled, strong, unyielding.

He licked the hollow of her throat and her head fell back. Yield. Yes, that was what she wanted to do. She still kept her knees tightly pressed together but now she did it because part of her wanted to let them fall open.

"Haley," he breathed, the word hot against her skin.

The sound of his voice made her shiver. He lifted his head and found her mouth. She wrapped her arms around him and clung as their passionate kiss swept her away.

She couldn't breathe, but then what did breath matter? She couldn't think, she could only feel the deep kisses. One of his hands settled on her waist. She felt the pressure, the heat, and when it began to move upward, she understood the destination.

Anticipation flooded her. Anticipation and need. Higher and higher he moved until finally he cupped her breast in his hand.

Time stood still. Haley didn't have the words or even the images to describe that feeling. His warm fingers, his palm holding her so delicately yet firmly. Then he brushed against her nipple. The sensation was so incredible, so unexpected, that she gasped a sound. Not a word but an unintelligible expression of her satisfaction.

He brushed her nipple again. She had to stop kissing so she could concentrate on the delight that coiled through her. She ached. She wanted more. She wanted everything.

Over and over he stroked, then he pinched the tight peak and she thought she might die from the wonder of it all. Again and again until the rhythm became the universe.

His other hand joined the first. They moved together. It was too much. It was wonderful. Unable to stop herself, she took his face in her hands and kissed him. She wanted all of him and when he entered her mouth, she sucked on his tongue, matching the movements of his fingers on her breasts.

Tension spiraled through her. It began in the center

of her body and moved lower to settle between her legs. She felt full, yet oddly empty.

Kevin broke the kiss. With his hands still on her breasts, he rested his forehead against hers.

"Okay, now it hurts," he said.

She opened her eyes and glanced down at his lap. His...maleness...seemed even larger than before. He looked very, very ready.

She raised her gaze to his face.

"Don't even think about it," he said, straightening and dropping his hands to his sides.

She hadn't decided if this was what she wanted or not, but having him tell her no before she could make up her own mind was a little annoying.

"Why do you get to decide?"

"Because both of us have to be willing."

"But you *are* willing."

"Physically, yes. But otherwise, no." He touched her cheek. "Not like this, Haley. Not in a motel on the highway with a guy you've only known a couple of days. The first time should be with someone you care about."

He spoke tenderly and his words brought tears to her eyes. He was right about all of it. Everyone had thought that Allan was a prince among men, but they'd been wrong. The injured man in front of her had turned out to be the most honorable person she'd ever met.

"I thought I loved Allan and I was wrong," she said. "How will I know when it's right?"

"You're asking the wrong guy. My track record stinks." He traced her lower lip with his thumb. "My mom always said I'd just know. Not very helpful, huh?''

Before she could respond, there was a loud beeping from the television. She turned and saw a red band at the bottom of the screen. The picture had switched from the ball game to a man standing in front of a weather chart. Kevin grabbed the remote and turned up the sound.

"Tornados have been seen in several counties,'' the man was saying, then he began listing them.

"I have no idea what county we're in,'' she said.

"Me, either.'' Kevin frowned at the map on the screen. "Isn't that the town we drove through earlier?''

"I think so.'' She glanced toward the window. "Are we going to be okay? Should we go to a shelter?''

Kevin wrapped his arm around her. "We'll be fine.''

"I've never been in a tornado.'' And she wasn't much interested in experiencing one now.

Kevin sighed heavily. "Go put on your pj's, then come back here. You can stay with me. We'll leave the TV on and monitor things.''

"You won't mind?'' She knew she would feel much better being in the same room with him.

"I'll take care of you,'' he promised.

She liked the sound of that because she wanted to take care of him, too. They could take care of each other. With Kevin that felt exactly right.

Chapter Nine

The next morning Haley found herself singing along with the car radio. She felt happy, light and in her best mood in days. The tornados had decided *not* to pay them a visit in the night, so she hadn't had to wrestle a mattress into the bathroom and fling herself and Kevin into the tub for safety. But she had spent the night in his arms.

Yes, it was true. Two nights out of the past four she'd slept with a man. And while he had made her drag in a sheet from her own bed so they didn't actually touch skin-to-skin, they'd been close enough for her to feel the heat of his body and to wake up with his arms around her and her head on his chest. It had been the absolute best morning ever.

She glanced at him out of the corner of her eye. He was sitting beside her in the passenger seat with his injured leg out straight, tapping his fingers in time with the upbeat country song. When he saw her looking at him, he gave her a slow, sexy smile that made her entire body shiver with delight. In a word—cool.

Kevin was something special. She'd started to figure that out the very first night when he'd refused to take advantage of her drunken invitations to kiss her and more. He'd been funny, gentle, kind, respectful and last night he'd managed to make her feel like a princess, even as he'd once again refused to take her to his bed. Well, he *had* taken her to his bed, but once the lights were out their activities had been strictly rated G.

Part of her understood his reluctance, even if she would never admit it. She supposed that making love with a twenty-five-year-old virgin was something of a responsibility. But what she couldn't seem to make Kevin understand was that she trusted him completely. His comment that she should care about the man before giving herself to him only made her trust him more. That bit about not doing it in a roadside motel hadn't made any sense. Location wasn't the point. But caring about the man—he was right with that.

What he didn't seem to get was that she cared about *him*. How could she not? He'd seen the truth about Allan in forty seconds and it had taken her nearly five years. He'd called Allan a jerk and had defended her. Kevin was the most amazing man she'd ever met. How was she supposed to resist him?

He thought she wanted to have sex just for the experience, but he was wrong. Okay, maybe things had started out that way. When she'd first hit the road, she'd been determined to be as bad as possible and part of that had been to find the right guy to show her what was what between a man and a woman. But somehow Haley didn't think she could have been with just anyone. And Kevin wasn't just anyone.

She found herself wanting to tell him things she'd never told another person. She wanted to hear all about his life and to be the keeper of his secrets. She wanted to spend time with him. She wanted to make love with him.

Just thinking about it made various body parts tingle. Somehow she was going to have to get him to see that she was more than just an innocent on the lookout for a life-altering experience. She and Kevin had a connection—one she couldn't explain. For all those years she'd thought she was in love with Allan, she'd never once felt the same bond.

Beside her, Kevin pulled out his cell phone. "When we get closer to Oklahoma City I should be able to get a stronger connection. I need to check in with my office. And I want to call my mom and let her know when to expect me." He glanced at her. "Anyone you need to call?"

"Not until tonight," she said, trying not to feel guilty.

When she knew everyone had left the church she would leave another message for her father, telling him that she was fine. She'd been gone a week—no doubt he was worried about her. As for what Allan might be feeling, she didn't want to know. She was still angry with him. To be honest, she was also angry with herself for not canceling the wedding months ago when she'd known she didn't love him and that getting married would be a mistake.

"Your father?" Kevin asked.

She tightened her hold on the steering wheel as she nodded.

"Where's your office?" she asked before he could question her further.

"D.C."

"What do you do there?"

"Not deliver prisoners." He shifted his leg a little to the left. "I picked the short straw this time."

"Is it usually dangerous?"

"Depends on who is being transported. This is the first time I got called back for a riot."

"When did you decide to go into law enforcement?"

Kevin considered the question. There hadn't been any one event that had sent him in that direction. "Sometimes I think I did it as a joke," he admitted. "I've told you that I was a screwup as a kid. My days in military school showed me a life I didn't want to be living. So I cleaned up my act. When I got to college, I looked around for a major. Criminal justice appealed to me. I figured I knew the bad guy's side of things, maybe it would be interesting to check out the other half."

"You must have liked it."

"I did. When I graduated, I knew I didn't want to go to law school. The Dallas police department had done some recruiting. I applied and they took me." He remembered his surprise when he'd been notified.

"I kept waiting for them to realize they'd made a mistake."

She glanced at him. "They didn't make a mistake. You were a good cop."

Typical Haley—always believing the best of him. "You don't know that."

She smiled. "Of course I do. You wouldn't have moved up to the Marshals if you'd been bad at law enforcement."

"Good point," he said wryly. "I did okay. Got a couple of promotions, then heard about the Marshals. I applied and they accepted me."

He'd spent the past several years waiting for *them* to find out the truth, but so far he had them all fooled. They still thought he was one of the good guys.

"My boss keeps offering me a promotion," he said without thinking.

"You say that like you've turned it down before."

"Yeah. Twice." Kevin rubbed his sore leg. "It's more of a desk job, coordinating fieldwork. I took the test for it, which was stupid. Or maybe passing was stupid." He didn't tell her that he'd aced it, coming in on top.

"Aren't you interested in a new challenge?"

He chuckled. That's exactly how Haley would view change—as a challenge. She was a lemons-to-lemonade, the glass-is-half-full kind of gal.

"I thought I was interested."

"So what's the problem? Are you afraid you'll miss being in the field all the time?"

"Maybe."

He felt uncomfortable and wished he hadn't

brought up the subject. When he had problems, he didn't like to talk about them with anyone. Instead, he worked them through on his own.

"That happens in the church," she said, and pulled on her sunglasses as the sun broke through the clouds and flooded the car with light.

Kevin put on his own glasses and tugged down the brim of his hat.

"Some missionaries head out into the world, do their three- or five-year tour, then come back. But others love what they do so much they make it their life's work. They can't adjust back to the 'regular' world, or they don't want to."

He understood the analogy, but knew that wasn't the problem. Sure fieldwork could be exciting, but mostly it was tedious and detail-oriented. TV cop dramas never showed all the grunt work that went into cracking a case.

"It's not that," he admitted slowly. The truth formed in his mind and he wondered if he could tell her. With anyone else, he would say no. But his gut said she would understand. Crazy, considering she was about the least sophisticated person he knew.

"I know what I am on the inside. One day they're going to find out, too, and then all this will be over."

He couldn't see her eyes, but the corner of her mouth twitched. "You think you're just a bad seed waiting to sprout again?"

"Sort of. I don't like the seed reference."

The twitch turned into a smile. "Would something more macho be preferable?"

"Yeah. Macho and dangerous. A seed? Come on."

"I can't think of anything better, sorry." Her smile faded a little. She glanced at him. "How long has it been since your last legal infraction or whatever you want to call it?"

He shrugged. "Fifteen, sixteen years."

"That's about half your life. If you were going to suddenly transform back into a menace to society, don't you think it would have happened by now? No one can avoid his real nature for very long. So either that isn't your nature or you have extraordinary skills in subjugating your evil side."

The simple truth of her words slammed into him like a speeding bullet. He turned the idea over in his mind, then mentally groaned. Well, hell.

He felt foolish, sheepish and relieved all at once. Damn if he hadn't been hiding from ghosts all these years. He'd been so caught up in his past, in the fear of what he *could* have been that he hadn't once thought about what he was. What he'd become.

"Pretty smart for a girl," he mumbled.

"Thank you." She wiggled in her seat. "Brains and beauty. However will you resist me?"

He was not going there. Resistance was hard enough without her bringing it up. "How'd you figure me out so easily?" he asked by way of shifting the subject. Most women told him he was emotionally inaccessible. Obviously, Haley didn't agree.

"I just saw who you were. From the first second we met, you've been nothing but kind and gentlemanly. How could I keep from believing in you?"

Her words make him both proud and apprehensive. He'd seen the light in her eyes when she looked at him and he didn't want to do anything to make it fade. But despite finally figuring out he was unlikely to start a life of crime at any second, he still wasn't the right guy for her. Reformed bad boys weren't known to be good relationship material.

"Don't make me into a hero," he warned.

"Too late. You became that the first night we met when you rescued me from those men and didn't take advantage of me. You cemented my opinion last night when you once again chose honor over, um, you know."

"'You know'?"

She sighed. "You're trying to get me to say the S-word and that isn't going to happen."

He chuckled, then turned serious. "I wouldn't take advantage of you, Haley. I couldn't."

She pulled off her sunglasses and glanced at him. The light was burning on high.

"I know," she said. "That's why you're one of the good guys."

As he looked at her, he felt something tugging in the center of his chest. A connection he'd only ever felt once before, with his twin brother. For years he and Nash had been close enough to be halves of the same whole. But as they'd grown up, that had changed. They'd separated, becoming their own persons. Kevin never thought he would feel that bond again.

Only this time it was different. His relationship with Haley wasn't brotherly. It was far more dangerous. Maybe for both of them.

Hands off, he told himself as she returned her attention to the road. If he was going to live up to her expectations of him, he would have to remember the rules. Rule number one: he would leave her as he'd found her.

Kevin checked his watch. It was just after three. "We can drive through, Mom," he said into his cell phone. "I'd be home late tonight."

"Don't even think about it," his mother told him firmly. "You've been shot. Your stepfather and I want to see you, but we'll wait until you arrive. Take it easy. You probably shouldn't be traveling in the first place, so I don't want you to push things."

Kevin thought about Haley's leisurely pace and the way she watched after him. "I'm in good hands. You don't need to worry."

He heard the smile in his mother's voice as she spoke. "I'm allowed to worry. It comes with having children. But I'll admit I worry a lot less than I used to."

After all he'd put her through in the years he'd spent growing up, she deserved a little peace of mind. "Then I'll see you in a couple of days. I love you, Mom."

"I love you, too. See you soon."

They said goodbye and hung up. Kevin tucked the cell phone back into his pocket and watched Haley walk out of the bathroom and head for their table. As she slid in across from him, she glanced at his empty plate.

"See. I told you it would be good."

She'd insisted they stop for afternoon dessert when

she'd seen the sign for homemade berry pie. For a skinny thing, she sure packed away the food. She'd ordered her pie with ice cream on the side and had polished off every bite. Not that he was in a position to cast stones, he'd done the same thing.

"You were right," he said. "It was homemade and delicious."

The café was straight out of the fifties, with red-vinyl bench seats in the booths along the front window and several counter seats up front. The waitresses wore pink uniforms with starched white aprons and the jukebox held real forty-fives. Currently Elvis was asking for someone to "Love Me Tender." The scratchy music made Kevin feel as though he was back in high school. Had that been the case, he would have slipped his letter jacket over Haley's shoulders so the whole world would know she was with him.

"Did you call your boss?" Haley asked, rearranging the condiments by the window.

"Uh-huh."

"And?"

She looked at him, her hazel-blue eyes wide with anticipation. So that was why she'd been gone for so long. She'd been giving him privacy.

He shrugged. "I told him I should be back at work in a couple of weeks."

Haley rolled her eyes. "I don't care about that. What did you say about the promotion?"

"I said I was interested."

She straightened and beamed at him, then thrust her hands across the table to clutch his. "Oh, Kevin, I'm so glad. You're going be terrific."

High praise considering she didn't even know what the promotion entailed. But that was Haley. For reasons he couldn't understand, she had total faith in him.

Her fingers pressed against his and she squeezed. The contact warmed him from the inside. Funny how after such a short period of time she could get to him. He found himself wanting to pull her close and hold her against him. Not for sex, although he still wanted her in his bed, but just to feel the beat of her heart. Being around Haley felt…right.

That thought scared the hell out of him so he released her hands and tossed a couple of bills onto the table to cover their check.

"Where do you want to spend the night?" he asked. "We could probably go another eighty miles before stopping."

Haley shook her head. "We have to stay here."

He glanced around at the café. The pie had been good, but not that good. "Why?"

She pointed out the window. He looked across the street, saw the sign and groaned.

"You're kidding," he said, even though he already knew she wasn't.

The large, sprawling wooden building looked like what it claimed to be—a country-western bar. The big marquee up front proclaimed Talent Night At Honky-Tonk Blues. The winner is promised fame and fortune. Or at least a hundred bucks in prize money.

He returned his attention to her. "You're not serious."

She nodded vigorously. "Absolutely. I play a mean piano. I could win."

Kevin slumped down in his seat. Hell. Just what he needed. Haley back in a bar and playing church tunes for a rowdy crowd.

The whole situation was worse than he'd thought, Kevin realized five hours later as he and Haley crossed from the motel they'd checked into and headed for Honky-Tonk Blues. Not only had the parking lot filled up with pickups and SUVs, but the sounds coming from the bar warned him the place was anything but quiet.

"Are you sure about this?" he asked Haley as he held open the wooden door.

She answered, but the words were pulverized by the wall of noise that slammed into them when he opened the second door.

They stepped into a pounding beat of music punctuated by loud conversation, rowdy laughter and plenty of cowboys who instantly gave Haley the once-over.

Kevin didn't have to glance back at her to remember she was dressed in a denim skirt that barely fell to mid-thigh, another of those damned cropped T-shirts and high-heeled strappy sandals that made her legs look endless. She was walking, breathing temptation.

But while she was in his company, she was his responsibility. So when a tall, skinny guy in a cowboy hat headed in their direction, Kevin grabbed Haley's hand and pulled her toward a table that had just been vacated by three women with big hair.

"You can still change your mind," he said when they were seated. He had to yell to be heard over the throbbing music.

Haley shook her head as she glanced around at the oversize room. He followed her gaze and saw couples moving together on a crowded dance floor. Behind them was the stage where a pretty decent band provided the noise and the rhythm. A bar lined the far wall. People were six deep waiting to be served. Banners hung down from the ceiling proclaiming tonight to be Talent Night.

"You ever play in a place like this?" he asked, even though he knew the answer.

"Not really. I've played in church, of course. And did recitals at school."

Figures. "So you didn't moonlight in a rock-and-roll band in high school?"

She looked at him and laughed. Her eyes lit up with humor and her soft mouth parted slightly. At that moment he wanted to kiss her more than he had wanted anything. He also wanted to whisk her away because there was no way she was going to be able to tame this crowd. He winced when he thought of the potential disaster.

"You don't have to do this," he said.

Her gaze narrowed. "You're right. I don't have to do anything. But I've spent the past twenty-five years doing what everyone else has told me to do. I think I'll spend the next twenty-five years doing just what I want."

He wasn't about to force her, so all he could do was flag a passing waitress and ask who they talked to about entering the contest.

Fifteen minutes later he'd finished a beer and was thinking that maybe he should have ordered something with more alcohol. Being drunk would take the edge off his tension, not to mention douse the ache in his leg. If he was drinking tonight, he wouldn't be taking any painkillers, which meant getting drunk had a lot of appeal.

Haley signed her name on the bottom of the release form and stood, prepared to head for the stage. There were going to be six acts tonight—she would be the last.

Kevin grabbed her wrist. "You okay?" he asked.

"No, but I'll survive."

"Don't go picking up any strange guys."

"As if," she said with a grin. "Besides, I don't want anyone but you."

Then, while he was still immobilized by her simple, honest and unexpected confession, she leaned forward and planted a quick kiss on his lips, turned and sashayed her way to the side entrance to the stage.

She'd managed to hit him right where he lived, and with just one sentence. He'd be laid low for a week if she ever worked up to full paragraphs.

Kevin noticed he wasn't the only male to catch the sway of her hips or the way her short blond hair bounced with each step. There was going to be trouble, he thought grimly, and he'd left his gun back in the room.

* * *

The first talent-show contestant seemed to be a regular. Several in the crowd called out greetings to the buxom redhead who carried a guitar onto the stage. When she was seated, the room went relatively quiet as she sang a couple of ballads.

Kevin ordered a second beer, then decided he'd better not drink it. He nursed a glass of water instead and sat through a lousy band, a magician who looked young enough to still be in grade school and two more singers who didn't have enough talent between them to fill up a shot glass. Then it was Haley's turn.

By this point, his nerves were stretched tight enough to *be* guitar strings. While the crowd had gone easy on the underaged magician, they'd hooted the band and both lousy singers off the stage without even letting them finish their two numbers. Haley was pretty enough to get the sympathy vote, but was that going to save her?

His muscles clenched tight the second she appeared on the stage. There were several whistles and catcalls as she walked to the piano that had been rolled out onto the middle of the stage. The man in charge adjusted a microphone so that it was level with her mouth. The house lights went down and a spotlight appeared on her.

"Hey, baby, why don't you show me another kind of talent?" one of the guys up front yelled.

Haley shaded her eyes against the glare of the spotlight, glanced at the man, then shook her head. "Thanks, but I'd rather play the piano."

The room exploded into laughter. Kevin relaxed a little. He didn't think Haley had understood what the guy had been talking about but she'd handled him perfectly.

"I haven't played in a while," she said, resting her hands on the keys. "Can I have a second to warm up?"

"I'm hot already, baby!"

Haley frowned slightly, then ran her fingers up and down in a quick series of scales. Kevin sensed people getting restless. She moved into a piece he didn't recognize but that sounded classical. He groaned. This wasn't the place for Bach.

A couple of people booed. Somebody yelled at her to get off the stage. Haley paused uncertainly. Kevin started to stand. If she needed rescuing, he wasn't going to let her down.

"Not your style, huh," she said, then shrugged. "I was trying to provide a little culture, but I guess not. Then how about this?"

At the first tinkle of the keys, Kevin froze. He didn't recognize that song, either, but it sounded like an intriguing combination of jazz and blue grass. As people began clapping, he sank back into his seat. He raised his beer in a silent salute. Looked as though Haley wasn't going to need rescuing at all. She was doing just fine on her own.

Haley lifted her hands from the keyboard and set them in her lap. There was a second of silence, followed by an explosion of applause. People yelled for her to keep on playing. She was about to shake her head no when she saw the nice man who had moved the piano onstage for her nodding at her to continue.

She started on another piece by a friend of hers from college, speeding it up a little and throwing in some country-sounding bass notes. If the dance floor had been crowded before, it was positively jammed now. She looked at the men and women moving together and started to smile. This was a lot more fun than playing at choir practice.

She stretched out the song, repeating the middle section. It had been so long since she'd played for pleasure that she'd nearly forgotten how much she really did like music. Somehow the piano had become part of the world she'd been trying to escape and she'd lost her joy in it.

Yet tonight she'd found it again. Her fingers moved with a lightness and confidence she'd never experienced before. It was almost as if she didn't have to think about the notes—they simply flowed from inside of her. She could have played for hours.

When the song ended, the nice man returned to stand next to her. He motioned for her to rise, then he took her hand and raised it in the air.

"We have a new winner!"

Everyone applauded. Haley couldn't believe it. "I won?"

"Sure thing, honey. Here." He handed her a hundred-dollar bill. "Feel free to spend it all here."

Haley laughed, then gave him an impulsive hug. She'd won!

After hurrying off the stage, she wove her way through the crowd, searching for Kevin. She wanted to show him the money. She also wanted to hear what he thought of her playing. Mostly she just wanted to be with him.

"Hey, not so fast."

Someone grabbed her wrist and swung her around. She found herself facing a dark-eyed man with a moustache.

"How 'bout I buy you a drink."

Haley smiled as she shook her head. "No thanks. I'm with somebody."

The man released her. "Then he's a lucky man."

Haley nodded and headed for the center of the room. She saw Kevin and waved. At that moment, her heart thudded against her rib cage in an unfamiliar rhythm. *I'm with somebody*. Weren't those the best words ever?

"You were terrific," Kevin said as she approached.

She hurried toward him, rushing the last few feet when he stood and opened his arms.

His embrace felt like coming home. The heat of him, the feel of his body, his scent, it all felt exactly right. She belonged here. Maybe it had only been a few days, but she was more comfortable with Kevin now than she'd ever been with Allan, or anyone else she'd met.

"You scared ten years off of me when you started with that classical music," he told her. "Then you blew my socks off. Pretty sneaky."

She waved the money in front of him. "And now I'm rich. Dinner's on me. Where do you want to go?"

His dark gaze settled on her face. At that moment something dangerous and fiery flashed in his eyes. Something that made her stomach clench and her legs tremble. Something that reminded her of them kissing the previous night.

Even with her limited experience, she recognized the look of a man who wanted a woman. But instead of saying anything about that, he wrapped his arm around her and said, "I think I have a taste for a burger. What about you?"

Haley didn't mind that he wouldn't admit his feelings. She agreed to a burger all the while knowing that they were in adjoining rooms and that it was the kind of night where anything could happen.

Chapter Ten

"You should have let me pay for dinner," Haley said as they walked toward their motel. "I wanted to."

"No way. Contest winnings are play money. Find something you would never let yourself buy and get it." He grinned. "Maybe one of those stuffed armadillos you're so fond of."

She wrinkled her nose. "I think they're interesting but I would never want one in my house. I'd always feel bad about it being dead."

"You wouldn't want a live one in the living room."

"Probably not."

Haley paused while Kevin pulled his room key out of his pocket. They were in adjoining rooms as they had been the previous night, but Haley was hoping that she wouldn't be sleeping alone. She'd liked sharing a bed with Kevin, even if he had kept his hands to himself.

He pushed open the door and motioned for her to go in first. She walked into the room and flipped on the light switch, then spun around in a circle.

"I still can't believe I won."

He smiled. "You did great. When you said you'd studied music for years, I didn't know it was anything like that."

"Oh, there were plenty of days spent on the classics, but sometimes we had fun. I'd nearly forgotten how much I enjoy music. I'm going to put playing just for pleasure on my to-do list."

He closed the door and tossed the key on the dresser. "You have a to-do list?"

"Uh-huh. It's all the things I want to do now that I'm free to follow my dreams." She began ticking items off on her fingers. "I'm going to play what I like on the piano. I'm going to visit Hawaii, and become a schoolteacher."

"What about winning a talent contest? Was that on the list?"

"Nope, just a bonus."

He sat on the bed and rubbed his thigh.

"Is it hurting?" she asked.

"Some. I had a beer, so I won't be taking a painkiller tonight."

"I have some over-the-counter stuff in my suitcase," she said. "You can take that."

He nodded gratefully. She studied the lines of pain around his eyes and mouth, the fading bruises on his face. If only she could do something to make him feel better.

"Okay. Let me go get the bottle and also the stuff to change your bandage. I'll be right back."

She hurried through the open adjoining door and into her room. After turning on a light, she unzipped her suitcase and fished out the bandages and antiseptic cream, along with a bottle of aspirin. Before returning to his room, she kicked off her sandals, then walked barefoot across the carpet.

Kevin was where she'd left him, still sitting on the side of the bed. She handed him the aspirin first, which he swallowed without water. She grimaced.

"How can you do that?"

"Practice."

The thought of that taste in her mouth made her shudder.

"Do you want me to change your bandage now or do you want to let the pain ease a bit first?"

"I can do it," he said, taking the supplies from her.

Haley blinked at him. "What do you mean?"

"I appreciate all you've done, but I don't need your help tonight."

He didn't sound angry as he spoke, and the words were polite enough, but she still felt as if he'd slapped her. Not need her help? But she'd always changed his bandage. Some of her fondest memories were of what had happened after.

Heat flared suddenly. Was that the problem? She'd made her interest in him very plain. Maybe he didn't like it. Maybe he didn't like her. After all, he'd turned her down enough times.

"I'm sorry," she said quickly. Her eyes burned with tears, although she didn't know why she would want to cry. She felt both hot and cold and very, very small. "I'll just—"

She motioned vaguely, then hurried back to her room.

"Haley, wait."

She didn't listen. Instead, she pushed the door between their rooms closed and looked for a place to hide.

There wasn't one. She was in a strange motel just outside Oklahoma City. All the pleasure of her win earlier that evening dissipated as if it had never been. Her stomach lurched, protesting what she'd had for dinner.

She should leave. She could get in her car and drive far, far away. Except then she would strand Kevin and she couldn't do that. She was supposed to take him home. All right—she would get him in the car and they could make it to Texas tonight.

She sank onto the bed and covered her face with her hands. She couldn't do that, either. He was injured and in pain. She couldn't ask him to sit in the car all night just because she'd realize she'd made a fool of herself by throwing herself at a man who wasn't interested.

She swallowed hard, still fighting the tears, but eventually they won. She was cold and lost and humiliated. All she could think of was how much she liked Kevin and how he didn't like her and how all of this was so much worse than Allan telling her he didn't want to marry her.

"Haley."

She looked up, then quickly wiped her cheeks when she saw Kevin standing just inside the adjoining door.

"How did you get in here?"

He held up the credit card he'd used to pop the door open. Her gaze flew to the dead bolt she hadn't bothered to latch, then back to him.

"Don't cry," he said, limping toward her.

"I'm not," she said automatically, even as fresh tears spilled down her cheeks. "I'm fine. Don't worry about me."

"I can't help doing that."

He sat next to her. She wanted to move away, but that seemed kind of childish. Worse, when he put his arm around her, she found she *couldn't* move because having him hold her felt too good. But wasn't he her problem to begin with? How could he be the solution?

He pulled her close. She resisted, determined to stay upright. He sighed and shifted back so he could face her.

"You don't understand," he said quietly. "I'm trying to be the good guy here and you're making it damned hard." He frowned. "What happened to your swearing lessons? I thought you were going to practice."

She sniffed. "I don't think I'm the swearing kind of person."

"Probably not." He took her hand in his and

turned it over so he could study her palm. "But I am. I'm a lot of things that you're not used to."

He turned her hand back and laced their fingers together, then looked at her face. "Women are easy for me. They always have been. They find me attractive and enjoy my company in bed."

She stiffened. Great. So not only was he not interested, she was one of a crowd. Her face burned even hotter. She tried to pull her hand away, but he didn't release her.

"Getting laid has never been the issue," he said.

She didn't know what to do with that information. "What's your point?"

"I told you the difference between making love and sex. Do you remember?"

She nodded.

He stared into her eyes. "I can find plenty of women for sex, but finding women to make love with—women who matter—well, that's a different story." He stroked the back of her hand with his thumb. "Maybe it's me. Maybe I'm shallow. Or maybe I just have bad luck. I can't seem to find women I really care about. After a while, just having sex isn't enough. I want to be with someone I respect and care about."

This time she jerked her hand free and clenched it against her stomach. Pain sliced through her. It was worse than she thought. Not only didn't he want her, he didn't even like or respect her.

"I see," she said, although the words hurt. It was as if her throat had been rubbed raw by the pain.

"No, you don't." He cupped her face in his hands.

''Dammit, Haley, I'm trying to tell you that I like and respect you *too much* to just have sex with you.''

Now she was really confused. ''But I like you, too. You said I should wait until I cared about someone, and I care about you. I don't understand. If you don't want me, then just tell me. I'm sorry I've been throwing myself at you. I never meant to make you uncomfortable. I thought—''

Her insides got all tight and she was afraid she was going to cry again. ''I thought you wanted me, too.''

Kevin let loose a string of swearwords he was pretty sure that Haley had never heard. She looked startled but didn't run for cover, which he guessed was something.

''I'm saying this all wrong,'' he told her.

The problem was, he didn't know how to say it right. His goal from the beginning had been to not hurt her. Yet he had. He could see it in her eyes, in the set of her mouth. He'd wounded her and all he'd been trying to do was be a good guy.

He sucked in a breath. ''This is all new to you,'' he said. ''You're on an adventure for the first time in your life. You're experiencing new things and that's great. I'm having a good time with you. I can't remember enjoying anything more. You're sweet and funny and you experience everything with your whole heart. There's no holding back. I admire that.''

Some of the pain faded from her eyes, but she still looked wary. ''And?''

''And I wonder how much of what you're feeling is about this being a new and exciting situation. I don't want you reacting without thinking of the consequences.''

He couldn't believe that a beautiful woman was throwing herself at him and he was trying to talk her out of it. He deserved the Moron of the Year award.

Haley stared at him for a long time, then nodded slowly. "You're afraid I'm more caught up in the moment than in you. That this is about the new experience, not who you are as a person."

Kevin didn't like the sound of that. It made him feel like a touchy-feely New Age tofu eater.

"I have enough regrets for two lifetimes," he said, sidestepping her comment. "I don't want you to have the same."

"I want to say that I won't, but things are happening so fast. Sometimes it's hard to catch my breath." She ducked her head. "I'm sorry I've been throwing myself at you. Guys get the 'no means no' lecture all the time and I've been guilty of ignoring what you were saying."

She was apologizing for coming on to him? Okay, now he *knew* they were in an alternate universe.

He brushed her cheek with the back of his hand. "No matter what happens or doesn't happen, never doubt that I've wanted you from the beginning."

She glanced at him from under her lashes. "Really? So it's okay for me to suggest stuff?"

He had a feeling he was going to regret agreeing to anything but he would rather walk on hot coals than hurt her again. "You can suggest all you want as long as I'm free to say no."

Was he really saying that? What the hell was wrong with this picture?

She straightened and smiled at him. "Okay. I won't ask for sex or anything, but can we sleep together tonight?"

They might be sharing a bed but Kevin knew he wasn't going to be sleeping. Not while he was hard enough to hammer nails into concrete.

He groaned softly and rested his forearm over his eyes. Why had he agreed to this? Sleeping, or not sleeping, with Haley was going to be pure torture. Maybe if he asked her nicely she would hit him on the head with a lamp and he could pass out. Even the headache that would follow would be better than the low and steady throbbing ache in his groin.

The pain cranked up about twenty percent when the adjoining door opened and she stepped into his bedroom. Her face was washed, her hair brushed and she'd replaced her sexy denim skirt and cropped T-shirt with a camisole and matching panties.

As she crossed the room, her small, perfect breasts moved in a way designed to make a dead man hot. His gaze slipped to her long, bare legs, then back to her face where happiness radiated with a light bright enough to blind.

"How's your leg?" she asked as she pulled back the covers and slid in next to him.

Instantly her sweet scent surrounded him. In a second he would feel her heat and he would be lucky if he didn't just explode right there.

"Kevin?"

Oh, yeah. ''The leg's fine.''

She eased next to him and rested her head on his shoulder. Her hand settled on his bare chest, burning his skin and making rational thought impossible. Every fiber of his being focused on mentally forcing her hand down and down and down. As if that was going to happen.

He glanced at her and found her looking at him. She smiled. His chest clenched in response as he realized he could look at her forever.

''Never settle,'' he told her. ''Whatever you do, Haley, don't accept second best. If the guy you're seeing isn't interested in what you want, then dump him and find someone who is. Only accept the best. That's what you deserve.''

''You mean, like Allan not wanting to go to Hawaii on our honeymoon?''

''Right.''

''Or the kid thing.''

He nodded, not wanting to think about the fact that she was on the Pill. Birth control wasn't going to be an issue for them because—

His brain froze. It wasn't his fault. Considering more than half his blood supply was otherwise occupied, he figured he'd been doing a fine job of communicating. But then she started moving her hand against his skin, rubbing her fingers against his chest, slipping back and forth…back and forth. He held in a groan. Why didn't she just shoot him?

Haley liked the feel of Kevin's warm skin and the way the hair on his chest tickled her fingers. He was so much more muscular than she was. She liked his scent, too, and the way he was warm and made her feel safe. He was really nice and good-looking. He had a good job.

"Why aren't you married?" she asked. "Why didn't you try again after that one time went wrong?"

"I never fell in love."

"Huh. I guess that's the same as wanting to be swept away. That's what I want."

He chuckled. "Guys don't want to be swept away. That's a chick thing."

She'd never thought of herself as a chick, but it was still kind of cool to be called one. "But it's still true. We want the same thing."

"Yeah. But don't tell anyone I said that."

She smiled, then closed her eyes and lost herself in the feel of his body next to hers. Certain body parts were tingling and aching in a way she now recognized. She was getting turned on.

The feelings made her both tense and completely relaxed. She liked knowing that being around Kevin made her hot, even as the realization made her blush.

She trailed her fingers from his chest to his stomach until she reached his belly button. She was so startled to come in contact with something that intimate that she momentarily froze. Which meant she didn't fight when Kevin shifted suddenly and flipped her onto her back.

She opened her eyes and looked up at him. His face was chiseled and strained. Tension pulled his mouth straight.

"What's wrong?" she asked. "Did I hurt you?"

"How far did you and Allan go? I know you're a

virgin, but what did he do? Touching, petting? First base? Third?''

His voice was low and hoarse. Haley didn't understand what was going on. ''We kissed, nothing more. And I don't really know about the bases. I mean, I know what people mean when they talk about them, but I don't know what happens at each base.''

In high school she'd overheard girls talking about what they let their boyfriends do, but she'd never been a part of a crowd that went further than chaste kisses.

Kevin squeezed his eyes shut. ''I'm going to hell,'' he muttered.

''No, you're not. You're a very good person.''

He opened his eyes. ''Honey, you don't have a clue what I'm thinking right now.''

Whatever it was, she wanted him to do it. The ache inside of her increased, as did the anticipation. She shifted to get closer. ''You could tell me.''

He groaned. ''You have no idea how much I want you.''

She nearly bounced with excitement. ''I want you, too. This isn't just about sex. I swear. I couldn't imagine doing this with someone else.''

''You were supposed to tell me no.''

''Oh. But I don't want to say no.''

''And I'm not ready to deal with you being a virgin.''

Which put them at an impasse. She didn't know what to say to that.

''I want to touch you,'' he said, ''but I won't make love with you. I plan to stop just short of that, even if it kills me. You can agree or if you've changed your mind, we can just go to sleep.''

Sleep? When the alternative was being touched by him? She didn't think so.

''Go for it,'' she whispered, and raised her head to kiss him.

The touch of his lips was as soft and perfect as she remembered. He leaned over her, his arm braced by her head, his body pressing against hers. As he moved back and forth against her mouth, she parted and his tongue slipped inside.

He tasted of toothpaste and heat. They came together in a dance that took her breath away. Everything was familiar yet new.

He explored her mouth, circling her, teasing her, making her squirm, then he broke the kiss and pressed his mouth to her jaw. She reached up and rubbed her hands along his bare back as he kissed his way to her ear, then took the lobe in his mouth and sucked. Tingles exploded like fireworks, arcing across the darkness of her passion.

He settled his hand on her stomach. The warm weight filled her with anticipation. But he didn't move, which made her want to grab his wrist and pull him up to her breasts.

He kissed her neck, licked the hollow of her throat, then blew on the damp spot and made her break out in goose bumps. But still that hand just sat there.

He raised his head. ''I'd like to take off your top.''

Embarrassment battled with desire. It wasn't much of a fight. Making love meant getting naked. While the thought of taking off her clothes even at the doctor's office made her want to hide under a desk, she didn't mind if Kevin saw her. Not when he looked at her with such tenderness and fire.

She scooted into a sitting position and reached for the hem of her camisole. With one quick move, she pulled it over her head and let it fall to the ground.

In case she managed to forget what she'd done, the cool night air was an instant reminder. She waited for him to look at her, to say something, but his gaze didn't leave her face. Instead, he tugged her back onto the mattress and kissed her again. His tongue swept into her mouth with all the power of a man on the prowl. She felt both feminine and vulnerable, but in a good way. In a jungle fantasy sort of way. And when his hand settled on her again, she had a feeling that this time he meant business.

She wasn't wrong. She felt the instant his hand slipped from the silky fabric of her tap pants to her bare stomach. Every cell went on alert. He moved high and higher until he settled over her left breast.

He'd touched her there before, but she'd been wearing her dress and nothing about that experience had prepared her for the liquid pleasure of having bare skin against bare skin. When he cupped her curves she couldn't breath. When he brushed his thumb against her tight nipple, she thought she might pass out. When he broke their kiss to lean down and take her nipple in his mouth, she knew that she had in fact left gravity behind and was now floating in the cosmos.

Warm, wet, sucking heat surrounded her. She hadn't known it could be like that, that she could be so sensitive, that she could feel this good. Ever. She gasped for breath and clutched at his head, never wanting him to stop.

He shifted to her other breast and used his fingers to mimic the movement of his tongue. It was too much. It would never be enough. It was endless…it was the most perfect moment in time.

She gave herself up to him then, not able to speak as he sat up and reached for her tap pants. Suddenly she wanted them off, too, because if he could make her breasts feel that good, imagine what would happen when he touched her there!

Then she was naked. Somehow Haley had thought the moment would be notable. That she would remember getting naked and feel that it was significant. But all it felt was right. When Kevin settled next to her again, he smiled.

"Have I told you how pretty you are?"

She shook her head.

"You are. Very pretty. Everything about you is lovely."

As he spoke, he rested his finger in the valley between her breasts, then moved it over one and then the other. He brushed against her nipple and when she gasped, he smiled again.

Those magic fingers trailed down her chest, then across her belly.

"I'll stop if you want," he said as he circled her belly button.

She still couldn't speak so she shook her head and even parted her legs a little, although that was kind of embarrassing. He moved lower, tickling as much as he excited. Heat flared ahead of his touch, making her feel as though she was melting from the inside out. When he slipped between her legs she felt several powerful jolts. She also realized she was slick and swollen. She glanced at Kevin to see if that was okay, but his eyes were closed. He went deeper, then groaned.

Questions filled her mind but before she could speak, he started kissing her again. Everything got very intense as he swept inside of her mouth, claiming her.

At the same time he moved his fingers as if he wanted to discover all of her. She liked the feel of him rubbing against her. It was just as nice as when he'd touched her breasts. Maybe nicer. Maybe—

Lightning shot through her. Haley wasn't sure what had happened but she wanted it to happen again. And then it did. He'd found this one incredible spot—this place that was so…

She gasped. Her legs fell open completely. Now she was the one to deepen their kisses. She wanted more. She wanted it all. Harder. Softer. Faster. Slower. She didn't care. Just as long as he was there, touching her like that.

It was like climbing and fall and floating all at the same time. When she realized her hips were pulsing in time with his movements, she didn't know how to make it stop. Then she didn't care. More. There had to be more.

He circled her sweet spot, brushed across it, then rubbed it again. The movements got faster. She couldn't breathe, but she didn't care. Breath wasn't required. There was so much to feel, to experience, and then suddenly it all rose so high that the world disappeared and there was only the sensation of rushing pleasure sweeping through her body over and over again until she returned to Kevin's arms.

She opened her eyes and found him watching her. "How was it?" he asked.

She couldn't believe it. She'd had an orgasm. Her first ever. Who had thought that up? "Amazing. Can we do it again?"

He laughed. "Sure, but if we do it right away, you'll be sore in the morning."

"Okay. We can wait."

He shifted onto his back and she cuddled next to him.

"Wow," she said, energized and ready to conquer new worlds. "I just had no idea I was capable of that. No wonder people run around doing it all the time."

"I've created a monster," he said.

"No, but you have unleashed my carnal nature." She snuggled closer, liking the way her bare breasts nestled against his arm. Then she shot up into a sitting position. "What about you?"

"I'm fine."

She narrowed her gaze, then flipped back the covers he'd kept over his lower half. The size of his arousal made her mouth drop open.

"Tell me what to do," she said.

"Don't worry about it." He reached for the covers.

She stopped him. "Why can't I make you feel good? Do you think I'll do it wrong?"

"No." He hesitated. "It's okay that this is just about you."

"But I want it to be about both of us."

"So much for being noble," he muttered, and reached for his briefs.

She watched as he pulled them off. He was careful as he slid them over his bandage. When he stretched out on the bed, she stared at him, at how big he was and, golly, if he didn't stick straight out, the way he'd promised.

She wanted to study his body, to explore their differences, but the strained look around his eyes told that he was a man on the edge. She would explore later, right now it was time for his orgasm.

"Okay, what do I do?"

He had her kneel next to him, then took her hand in his and wrapped it around him. He was hot, hard, yet the skin was so soft.

"Up and down," he said through slightly clenched teeth. "It's not going to take long." He looked at her. "You know what happens to men when they—"

She nodded. That much was clear to her.

He taught her the rhythm, then dropped his hand to his side. His eyes closed and as she moved she could see the tension tightening his body.

She liked how he filled her hand and the way he groaned as she quickened the pace. It felt as if she'd just gotten the hang of things when he stiffened and climaxed. Haley watched all of it, amazed at what she'd been able to do. Winning a talent contest, having her first orgasm and pleasuring Kevin all in one night. Life had just gotten very good.

Chapter Eleven

As Haley finished dressing she tried not to notice the look of apprehension in her eyes every time she glanced in the bathroom mirror. She wasn't nervous exactly, she just didn't know what was going to happen next.

Last night had been…spectacular. The things Kevin had done to her and that she had done to him had made her feel happy and alive and very connected to him. They'd fallen asleep holding each other and had awakened the same way. But he was still sleeping when she'd slipped out of bed to duck into her own room for a shower and she wasn't exactly sure about morning-after protocol. Did they talk about it? Did they not talk about it? Would things be awkward and icky?

She didn't want that. However wonderful things

had been in bed, she didn't want what they had the rest of the time to change. In the past few days Kevin had become very important to her. She liked being around him and talking to him. They were good together.

Haley pulled on her socks and shoes, then turned her attention to her short hair. As there wasn't much she could do with the mussed style, she ran a comb through the damp strands, then put on mascara and lip gloss.

Somehow she and Kevin had become a team, she thought as she packed her shampoo into a clear plastic bag. Had her eagerness to experience life on the wild side ruined that?

She stepped out into her room and came to a stop when she saw Kevin sitting on her bed. He was dressed and obviously ready to go, but she couldn't read his expression. Before she could ask how he was—how *they* were—he rose and crossed to her, then pulled her into his arms.

He felt as warm and strong as she remembered and when he kissed her, all her fears melted away.

"Morning," he said when he pulled back a little and gazed into her eyes. "How are you feeling?"

"Good."

He grinned. "Just good? Not amazing?"

"That, too."

"I'm glad." He studied her. "No second thoughts?"

"No."

He picked up her free hand and kissed her knuckles, then led her to the bed. When she was settled next to him, he turned serious.

"I want to push through to Possum Landing today," he said. "I know we talked about spending the night in Dallas, but I can't stay in a hotel with you, Haley. We both know what will happen."

She didn't know what to think. While part of her knew he was right, another part of her wanted to scream in protest. She wasn't ready to let him go. It was too soon. She hadn't prepared. Kevin had become so important to her. Was she just supposed to walk away without any warning?

He squeezed her free hand. "This may sound a little strange, but I'd like you to stay with me at my folks' house. Just for a couple of days. I don't want to get in the way of your travel plans, but…" He shrugged. "I guess what I'm trying to say is that I'd like to spend some more time with you."

Her panic faded, replaced with a contentment so powerful she practically purred. "I'd like that, too."

"I won't be keeping you from your drive to Hawaii?"

"The islands will still be there when I head out."

"Good." He rose. "I'm starved. Let's go get some breakfast before we hit the road."

She nodded and dropped her makeup bag onto the bed, then took the hand he offered and followed him out of the room. As they stepped into the clear, warm morning, Haley suddenly remembered something her father had said a long time ago.

She'd probably been ten or eleven and had been talking to him about why he'd never remarried. He'd explained that he'd loved her mother so much that just being in the same room with her, not doing anything special, was better than the most exciting party with anyone else. At the time she hadn't understood his point, but suddenly it all made sense. She would rather have breakfast at a diner on the highway with Kevin than tour Europe with another man. Given the choice—

Haley's thoughts shifted as she felt an unexpected stab of longing. For the first time since running away, she missed her father. She wanted to see him and to talk to him, to tell him about her adventures—okay, maybe not *all* of them. She wanted to hear his voice and to have him meet Kevin. She wanted him to say that he still loved her.

"You all right?" Kevin asked.

She glanced at him. "I'm fine. Just thinking about my dad."

"Want to use my cell phone to call him?"

She shook her head. "Maybe later." When she'd figured out what she was going to say.

"Are you sure this is okay?" Haley asked for about the four thousandth time.

"How often do I have to say yes?" Kevin asked.

"I don't know. I'll let you know when I stop being nervous."

They'd left the interstate about an hour ago and were now on the outskirts of Possum Landing. Haley glanced around at the well-maintained houses and tidy lawns and tried not to notice the rock sitting in her stomach.

This was crazy. "I should check into a motel," she said. "I can't stay at your house."

Kevin grinned at her. "Technically, it's not my house. It belongs to my mom and Howard."

She tightened her grip on the steering wheel. "And that makes it better?"

"It doesn't make it worse." He touched her arm. "Relax. I talked to my mom and she's happy to have you stay with us. You heard my half of the conversation. Did it sound like anything bad?"

"No, but..."

But wasn't it weird that he was taking her home with him? It wasn't as if she were an old college friend, or even a lost dog he'd picked up somewhere.

"Turn here," he said, directing her.

She came to a stop at the light, then turned right. Possum Landing reminded her a lot of her hometown, she thought, feeling more miserable by the minute. She half expected to start recognizing people. Which made her feel really guilty about having run away in the first place, and not having called and actually spoken with her dad.

Kevin led her into the homey-looking neighborhood. Guilt and nerves grew by the second. When they finally came to a stop in front of a large, two-story house, Haley didn't know if she was going to throw up or simply expire from the stress.

"Ready?" Kevin asked as he pushed open the passenger door.

She wanted to say no, but before she could speak, the front door of the house opened and two people stepped out onto the wide front porch.

Haley didn't remember getting out of the car, yet suddenly she was standing on the sidewalk being introduced to Kevin's parents. She thought she might have spoken, smiled and shaken hands, but the moment was just a blur of impressions and terror.

Kevin's mother, Vivian, looked far too young to have thirty-one-year-old twins. Even knowing she'd given birth to them when she'd been seventeen, Haley thought she looked fabulous. Tall and slender, with thick dark hair and cat-green eyes, she was as attractive as her son was handsome. Howard was a few years old, balding, with a friendly face and an air of a man who is comfortable with himself in the world.

After greeting her, Vivian and Howard turned to Kevin and hugged him. His mother cupped his face and looked more than a little worried, while Howard fussed over his cane.

"I can't believe you were shot," Vivian said as she led them to the house.

"Me, either." Kevin could walk without his cane, but when Howard handed it to him, he took it and used it without saying anything.

"Any side effects from that blow to the head?" Howard asked. He got to the front door first and held it open. "Should we call Doc Williams?"

"I'm fine," Kevin insisted with a grin. "We'll all go square dancing tonight and I'll prove it."

He waited for Haley to go in front of him. As she passed him, he winked at her.

Inside, the house was tastefully decorated in earth tones. Family pictures were scattered around on tables and shelves. Haley saw a much younger Kevin with a boy about the same age. His fraternal twin, she thought, liking Nash's broad smile and the glint in his eye.

"You tired?" Howard asked Kevin. "You can lie down before dinner if you like."

"Thanks, but all I did today was sit. Haley did the driving."

"Then I'll go get the suitcases." Howard headed for the front door.

"Oh, I'm only using the brown one," Haley said, remembering the several large suitcases in her trunk. "Kevin's is the duffel bag."

Kevin eyed the stairs. "I'm not looking forward to climbing those."

"Do you want to sleep on the pullout sofa?" his mother asked.

"No. I can make it. Just ignore the groaning."

Vivian looked more than a little worried as she studied her son. He wrapped an arm around her and squeezed.

"I'm fine," he insisted. "Stop fretting. I'm here, I'm upright and I'm not bleeding. Didn't you always say that was the best you could hope for with me?"

"In the past few years, I've raised my expectations."

He grinned. "Big mistake." He released her and gave her a little nudge. "Why don't you show Haley her room? I'm sure she'll appreciate that handmade quilt you bought a whole lot more than Nash and I did."

Vivian touched his cheek. "It's good to have you home."

"I'm happy to be here."

Haley watched the two of them together and felt the love that flowed between them. She hadn't much thought about Kevin's relationship with his family, but if someone had asked, she would have assumed it was strong. Having that confirmed made her feel warm inside.

"You must make yourself at home," Vivian said as she turned her attention to Haley and motioned to the stairs. "The guest room was redone a couple of years ago, so I hope you'll be comfortable."

"I'm sure it's lovely," Haley said. She quickly glanced at Kevin over her shoulder before following her hostess upstairs. He gave her a thumbs-up.

"You've been so kind to take me in," Haley said when she figured she was out of earshot. "I would really be fine at a motel."

"Nonsense." Vivian turned left at the top of the landing. "Howard and I rattle around this old place. If the bonus room didn't have the television in it, we wouldn't even get up here very often. Our bedroom is downstairs."

She paused in front of an open door. "Here you go."

Haley moved into a bright, cheery room filled with a queen-size bed, a white desk and double dresser. The quilt was done in yellows and blues and matching curtains hung at the wide window that faced the rear of the property.

"The bathroom is across the hall," Vivian said, "but you won't have to share. Nash and Kevin each have their own room with a bathroom in between."

"It's very nice," Haley said sincerely. She heard voices downstairs and assumed Howard had returned with the luggage. She expected Vivian to go to the stop of the stairs and call him, but Kevin's mother only leaned against the door frame and studied her.

"Thank you for bringing Kevin home," she said. "Knowing him, he would have started driving before he should have and probably made his injuries worse."

"I was happy to help."

More than happy. The past few days had been the most incredible of her life.

Vivian's green eyes darkened slightly. "I don't mean to pry, except I'm going to." She smiled. "I'm curious about your relationship with my son."

Haley felt heat on her cheeks and had a bad feeling she was blushing. Oh, no. "Um, what do you mean?"

Vivian shrugged. "He was never one to bring a girl home. I suppose he was always too much of a troublemaker for that. He would rather have been out racing cars or cutting school than court a girl. Of course, he's grown up. Women have become more interesting and cars less so. Are you two just friends or can we hope for something more?"

Haley had not idea how to answer that question. She desperately willed Howard to appear with the luggage, but he didn't, which left her with an empty silence to fill.

"We, ah…" She cleared her throat. "I guess we're friends." Did friends do what they'd done last night? "I like Kevin very much. He's a wonderful man."

"I think so, but then, I'm his mother. What else

would I say?'' She straightened. ''I won't grill you any more. Just know that we're very happy to have you here. Dinner is at six.'' She glanced at her watch. ''Which means I need to get cooking.''

''May I help?''

''We're just having a lasagna I took out of the freezer and salad. Unfortunately, Howard and I have to go out tonight.'' She wrinkled her nose. ''I hate to be gone on Kevin's first night back, but our bowling team is in the county championships and we can't miss.''

''He'll understand,'' Haley told her.

Vivian smiled. ''Plus he'll have you for company.''

She turned and walked down the hall. Haley watched her go. At least Kevin's mother didn't seem to mind that he'd brought her home with him. And she liked knowing that he hadn't brought other women to the house. It made her feel special—which happened pretty much any time she and Kevin were together.

''You wouldn't believe how much trouble one dog could cause,'' Vivian was saying. ''Still, with freshly planted shrubs, a good rain and sharp claws, he created a disaster. Mrs. Wilbur went after him with a rake. Chased him right down the center of the street.''

Kevin chuckled. ''Tell me the dog got away.''

''Of course he did,'' Howard said, taking a second serving of salad. ''She was spitting mad for weeks.''

Haley listened to them talk over dinner. They'd brought Kevin up to date on the goings-on around town while he'd been gone. As everyone seemed to know everyone else's business, she was reminded of home again. It was that way for her and her father. They often spent dinners talking about what dog got loose and what ten-year-old had fallen out of a tree and broken his arm.

Kevin stretched back in his chair and patted his stomach. "Haley and I have had some fine meals on the road, but nobody beats your lasagna, Mom."

She smiled her thanks. "You'd think it would be good enough to tempt you home more often."

He held up his hands. "Give me another twenty-four hours before you light into me about that."

"Fair enough." She sighed. "It's just good to have you here now."

Howard nodded his agreement.

"So what's the big news you didn't want to tell me by phone?" Kevin asked.

Vivian and Howard glanced at each other. In the look that flashed between them, Haley saw silent communication that spoke of love and trust and many wonderful years together. She turned away, as if she'd glimpsed something intimate and private. But married people shared looks like that all the time. Even couples who were just dating connected like that.

But not her and Allan, she thought. They'd never connected at all. She sat up a little straighter as she realized that in all the time she'd been gone, she hadn't once missed him. She'd thought about him but only as someone she'd managed to escape. Despite the small diamond ring she'd left on her dresser when she'd fled, she'd never loved him. Not even a little.

"Let's talk in the morning," Vivian said, interrupting Haley's thoughts. ''After that, we'll go visit with Edie.''

Kevin hesitated, then nodded. He turned to Haley. ''Edie Reynolds has been a friend of the family since before Nash and I were born. Her oldest, Gage, is the same age as Nash and me. Quinn is just a year younger. The four of us grew up together, more like brothers than friends.''

Howard glanced at his watch. ''We need to get going.''

Vivian motioned to the table. ''You have to give me a minute.''

''I'll clean up,'' Haley said quickly. ''It's the least I can do.''

Vivian looked as if she was going to protest, but Kevin told her to head on out. ''I'll supervise Haley so she does the job right,'' he promised.

His mother laughed, then kissed his cheek. The couple waved as they picked up matching bowling bags and hurried out the back door.

Kevin watched them go. ''Why didn't she tell me tonight?'' he asked when they were alone.

Haley didn't have a good answer. ''Maybe because they were rushed. Maybe she didn't want to say whatever it was and then have to leave.'' She looked at him. ''Are you worried?''

''No, but I could be.'' He shook his head. ''Whatever it is, she'll tell me in the morning. In the meantime, let's get the dishes done, then we can head upstairs and you can flip through the cable channels. Or we can watch a movie.''

''Either,'' she said, just happy to be with him.

He rose, but instead of picking up a plate, he helped her to her feet and pulled her close. "You doing okay with my folks?"

She nodded. "They're great."

He brushed his mouth against hers. "What about me?"

"You're great, too."

He winked at her. "I know."

Kevin tried to sleep, but he couldn't. Maybe it was because he was by himself instead of with Haley. After cleaning up, they'd watched a movie, then he'd sent her off to bed before their occasional kisses turned into something more dangerous.

He sat up, reached for his jeans and pulled them on, along with a T-shirt. Then he quietly limped down the hall to the stairs.

When he reached the main floor, he headed for the kitchen. His mom always kept cookies in the teapot-shaped cookie jar he and Nash had bought her for Mother's Day about twenty years ago. He smiled as he remembered pooling resources with his brother and then arguing about what to buy.

Headlights swept across the kitchen window as he poured himself a glass of milk and settled at the table. A couple of minutes later, his mom and Howard stepped inside.

"You're up late," his mother said when she caught sight of him. "Is your leg hurting?"

He shrugged. "No more than usual. How did it go?"

Howard held up a gaudy trophy. "Second place. Not bad for a couple of old folks."

"Congratulations."

His mother set her bowling bag on the floor. "Want some company for your snack?"

"Sure." He passed her the plate of cookies.

She took one but didn't eat it. Instead, she set it on the table and stared at him. "You want to talk about it now, don't you?"

Kevin shrugged. "I'm not doing anything else."

Howard patted his wife's arm. "I'll be in our bedroom when you're done."

Kevin was surprised that he left, but his mother's expression told him that they'd already discussed this and had decided she would be the one to tell him whatever she had to say.

He tried to shake off the uneasy feeling, but it wouldn't budge. The cookies stopped tasting so good.

"You said you weren't sick," he reminded her.

"I'm not. It's nothing like that." Vivian laced her fingers together. "Actually this is about your biological father."

Kevin had been braced for a number of different topics, but not that one. "What about him? He's a jerk."

He was a whole lot worse than that, but Kevin knew how his mother felt about swearing. Besides, there weren't enough bad words around to describe a man seducing a seventeen-year-old, getting her pregnant and then abandoning her.

His mother smiled. "I've always appreciated your

support. Nash's, too. You boys never blamed me for what happened.''

''That's because it's not your fault. You were a kid. He's the one to blame.''

''I know. I tell myself that. I thought I was so in love with Earl Haynes. He was handsome and funny.''

Kevin thought he was more of a bastard, but he didn't say that.

His mother sighed. ''What I never told you was I went to see him again. The following year. I found out he was returning to Dallas for the convention. My parents had just thrown me out and I didn't know what else to do. I thought if I explained what had happened he would help.''

Kevin leaned back in his chair. His muscles tensed as he prepared to hear something that would make him want to send the guy through the windshield of a car.

''Let me guess,'' he said. ''He blew you off.''

''Sort of. When I knocked on his hotel room, I interrupted him entertaining another woman. I was crushed. I'd thought it was love and I found out it wasn't. Worse, he claimed you boys weren't his and he said I hadn't been interesting enough to stay in touch with.''

His mother shook her head. ''I still remember how much it all hurt. I found my way to the lobby, but I was crying too hard to leave. I could feel people looking at me. I had nowhere to go, no money. I didn't know anything about social services or getting help. Then someone spoke to me. When I looked up, I saw the woman who had been in Earl's hotel room. I'd never seen her before, but she took me under her wing. We spent the morning together, sharing sad stories about Earl.''

''He'd seduced her, too?''

''Sort of. She was a little older and married. It seems her husband couldn't have children. They couldn't afford cutting-edge reproductive treatment. Don't forget this was over thirty years ago. Things weren't as advanced as they are today. Her husband wanted her to find someone who looked like him and get pregnant.''

Kevin flinched. ''That's barbaric.''

''She wasn't too happy about it, either. Eventually she agreed and headed up to Dallas where she met Earl the same weekend I did, the year before. He was real busy. We both got pregnant. The problem started when she realized she'd fallen in love with him. She came back to him, much as I had. They fell into bed again. That's where I found them.''

She shrugged. ''I would have been lost without her. She brought me here and helped me get a job and an apartment. It was her idea to create a fake dead husband so people wouldn't look down on me or you and your brother. When she found out she was pregnant a second time, her husband wasn't happy. They almost split up over it.''

Kevin's bad feeling had been growing with the telling. There was one piece of information his mother hadn't told him and he was starting to think it was damned significant.

''Who's the woman?'' he asked.

"Edie Reynolds."

The name slammed into him with all the force the bullet has used. Edie Reynolds? The woman he'd known all of his life and thought of as a member of the family? Her sons—Gage and Quinn... The four of them had been inseparable.

"Your brothers," his mother said, just in case he hadn't figured it out. "Actually, your half brothers. I never told you before because Edie didn't want her boys to know. Don't forget she was passing them off as Ralph's children. You knew your biological father had abandoned us and that was all that mattered."

He was having trouble absorbing all this. "What changed?"

"Gage found out the truth, so I knew it was time to tell you who your father really was and that your two best friends were really your half brothers."

Chapter Twelve

Kevin sat up well past midnight. His mother had long since gone to bed, although he doubted she would get much sleep. Telling him would have upset her almost as much as hearing the news had bothered him.

He tried to convince himself that nothing much had changed. He was who he had always been. His biological father was the same bastard he'd been two hours ago. Yet everything felt different. Gage and Quinn were his half brothers. They always had been. Why hadn't he seen it?

A soft creaking on the stairs broke into his thoughts. He turned toward the doorway and saw Haley tiptoe into the kitchen.

He took in her mussed hair and wide eyes. At least she'd stopped to pull on jeans and a T-shirt. He didn't think he could have resisted her in one of her sexy pj outfits. Despite the confusion he felt about a lot of things, he still wanted her.

"Couldn't sleep?" he asked.

She took the seat next to his and shrugged. "I was worried about you. I heard you go downstairs, and then your parents came home. I thought maybe you were talking about whatever your mom had to tell you and when you didn't come up to bed, I wondered if you were okay."

Her pale face was beautiful, her expression so damned earnest that it made him ache inside. Haley didn't have the life experience of a gnat, but still she worried about him and wanted to help.

"I'm fine," he said, taking her hand in his. "Confused, but fine."

"Do you want to talk about it?"

"Sure." He didn't mind her knowing. He'd already told her the worst about his past and had yet to shake her good opinion of him.

"My mom wanted to talk about the guy who got her pregnant with Nash and me. It seems he was more of a jerk than I'd realized."

He outlined what his mother had said, explaining how Edie Reynolds had been the one responsible for bringing his teenage mother to Possum Landing and helping her start over.

"I've known Gage and Quinn all my life," he said. "We played together, fought together, grew up and never guessed we were brothers."

"You must be happy having them as a part of your family."

"Why do you say that?"

She smiled. "Because family is so important. More is always better. Having people around who care about you and want you to do well. I would think that after being good friends all your lives, you would be happy to know there was an even deeper connection."

"Do you ever *not* see the bright side of things? I swear you could look at a pile of trash on the highway and claim it was modern art."

Her mouth trembled at the corners. "Is that bad?"

"No." He squeezed her fingers. "It's exactly as it should be."

He didn't want to figure out the reasons why, but he liked Haley seeing the world as a good and honest place. Maybe her thinking the best of people allowed him to believe that she saw the best in him. Maybe it wasn't all a crock.

"What happens now?" Haley asked.

"I'm going to talk to Gage tomorrow, and his mother. I guess I should get in touch with Nash, too."

She leaned toward him. "Are you sad about your dad? About what he did?"

He shrugged. "I made peace with what he did a long time ago. As far as I'm concerned, he was simply the DNA provider. When Nash and I were young, we didn't think much about having a dad. By the time my mom met Howard, we were old enough to appreciate having another guy in the house. He's the only father either of us has ever known. He's a great guy. He was always there for me when I was screwing up."

The grandfather clock in the living room chimed the hour. Kevin released Haley's hand. "It's late. We should be in bed."

Her eyes widened but before she could say anything, he shook his head. "Alone, Haley. You're going to your room and I'm going to mine."

"I knew that."

"Right."

He rose and pulled her to her feet. When she was standing, he kissed her. "For a good girl, you're sure doing your best to lead me down the path of being bad."

"For a reformed bad boy, you're certainly resisting."

He kissed her again, enjoying both the taste of her and the fire that flared to life in his groin. Wanting her felt good, even though he knew he wasn't going have her.

They walked to the stairs together, then he followed her up to the landing. Once there, he gave her a push in the right direction and watched as she entered the guest room. He thought about following her inside and what would happen. Funny that as much as he wanted to make love with her, he also enjoyed just being with her. Haley might be ten kinds of trouble, but she was also one of the best things that had ever happened to him. In a short period of time, she'd become a part of his world and he didn't want to think about how much he was going to miss her when it came time to let her go.

"What do you think about all this?" Kevin asked Gage the following morning. Edie and Vivian were still talking in the living room while he and Gage had gone out onto the porch.

"It took some getting used to," Gage admitted. He leaned one foot against the railing. "You always had an idea of who your real father was, but until a few weeks ago, I'd never heard of Earl Haynes."

Kevin studied the man he'd known all his life. Last night Gage had been a good friend, but now he was his brother. The information made him realize that he and Gage were about the same height, with similar coloring. In fact all four of them were tall, with dark hair, dark eyes. Gage's khaki sheriff's uniform emphasized broad shoulders similar to Kevin's. Hell, the proof had been there all along. None of them had ever thought to look for it.

"What happens now?" Kevin asked. "Did you tell Quinn?"

"I have a message out for him to call me. It could be weeks before I hear back from him. You getting in touch with Nash?"

"Yeah."

Gage looked out toward the yard. "Kari and I are heading to California. From what I could find out, Earl Haynes has several sons living out there. I guess they're our half brothers."

Kevin hadn't thought of other family, but it made sense. "Want some company?"

His friend grinned. "Sure thing. As long as you don't mind the mushy stuff. Kari and I are still at the crazy-in-love stage."

"I won't watch."

Kevin meant the comment as a joke, but as he spoke the words he realized something inside his chest ached. Gage was engaged and while he was happy for his friend, he also felt a little envious.

No way, Kevin thought, shaking off the feeling. He wasn't the kind of guy who wanted to get tied down. He'd considered it once and it had been a disaster. Long-term relationships weren't for him.

"Are you going to warn the California Haynes family that we're coming?" Kevin asked.

"I haven't decided. I don't know what kind of reception we'll get there. Maybe I'll try to contact them through e-mail. I was thinking we'd head out at the end of next month. I can get some time off then."

Kevin had more than enough vacation time due him. "That works for me."

The front door opened and his mother walked out. "Are you two about finished?"

Kevin and Gage looked at each other, then nodded. "I'll be in touch," Kevin said. They shook hands.

Gage studied him. "I can't help thinking we should have known."

"Me, too."

"We know now."

Kevin nodded. He thought about what Haley had said about being happy to have more relatives. At the time he hadn't understood, but now he did. He was glad to know that Gage and Quinn were members of his family.

"Are you all right?" his mother asked as they drove back to the house. "I know this has been a lot to take in."

"It's been a lot easier for me than for Gage. I've always known about my biological father."

"At least he has Kari to help him. You know they're engaged."

"I heard."

Kevin figured his mother was trying to be subtle, but he could see her coming a mile down the road. He braced himself for the inevitable questions.

"Haley seems very nice," she said right on cue.

"She is."

Vivian glanced at him and smiled. "Want to talk about it? It wouldn't kill you to tell me what's going on between the two of you."

"If I had a clue, I'd tell you everything." At least that was honest. He sighed. "Haley's very special, but she's not like anyone I've ever met. She's lived a sheltered life and until now, she hasn't seen much of the world."

"Are you concerned that the two of you are too different in that respect?"

"It's crossed my mind."

"Is it possible that you're thinking of settling down?"

Trust his mom to cut right to the chase. He opened his mouth to give his standard response, which was that he would get married when hell froze over, then reconsidered. There was no way that he and Haley could ever have anything permanent. He was a hundred percent the wrong man for her. But was she the right woman for him?

"I can't say how things are going with the two of us," he told his mother.

She smiled. "Can't or won't say?"

"You make me crazy."

She laughed. "I know. It's one of my favorite ways to spend an afternoon—paying you back for all the gray hairs I'm going to get."

Haley paced through the empty house. Kevin and his mother had left to visit with Edie and Gage Reynolds, and Howard was at work. She was alone and she knew exactly what she should be doing. The thing was, she didn't want to.

"He's my father," she whispered as she paused by the phone in the kitchen. "I shouldn't be afraid to call him."

She wasn't…not exactly.

She reached for the phone, then dropped her hand to her side. "This is stupid," she muttered, and picked up the receiver.

The connection went through quickly and before she was ready, she head a familiar voice say, "Pastor Foster's office. This is Marie."

Haley sucked in a breath and did her best to ignore the sudden burning in her eyes.

"Hi, Marie."

The woman on the phone gasped. "Haley? Is that you? Child, we've all be frantic with worry. Where are you? Are you all right?"

"I'm fine." Haley pulled out a kitchen chair and sank onto the seat. "I've left my dad a few messages saying everything was okay."

"Even so. Oh, Haley, he's going to be so happy to

hear from you. Hold on one second. Don't you go anywhere.''

There was a brief silence, then she heard her father's deep voice. ''Haley? Is that really you?''

Tears filled her eyes. ''Yes, Daddy. I wanted to let you know that I'm alive and well. I'm sorry I worried you.''

He sighed. ''Worry doesn't begin to describe it.''

He hadn't said anything mean or judgmental, but still she felt guilty. ''I just needed to get away for a while so I could think things through.''

''Where are you? When are you coming home? You should be here, Haley, with the people who love you.''

''I can't,'' she said as the tears spilled down her cheeks. ''Not yet, Daddy. Things happened.''

He sighed. ''I know all about 'things.' Allan told me everything.''

Somehow she doubted that.

''You need to understand,'' her father continued. ''Everyone gets last-minute jitters. I was surprised when Allan admitted to them, but his honesty impressed me. We've had a lot of talks and his mind is clear. He loves you and very much wants to marry you.''

Somehow that didn't make Haley feel any better. If she hadn't already figured out that she'd never been in love with Allan her lack of relief would have been a big clue. She didn't want to know that he was now willing to marry her. She didn't want anything to do with him.

''The problem is a lot bigger than last-minute jitters,'' she said. ''I don't love him, Daddy. I went out with him because it's what everyone wanted. I think I got engaged for the same reason. He's a very nice man but he's not the one for me.''

He wasn't Kevin, she realized. Kevin who made her heart beat faster just by walking in the room. Kevin who treated her as if she were the most precious woman in the world. Kevin who made her laugh and listened to her opinion and believed she could do anything she wanted.

''You don't know what you're saying,'' her father told her. ''Haley, you've never been very good at making your own choices. Hold on a minute.''

Outrage erupted inside of her but before she could vent, there was a click and the sound of a voice she didn't want to hear.

''Hello, Haley.''

This is why she hadn't wanted to talk to her father. He loved her, but he didn't listen. He'd never listened.

''Allan.''

Her ex-fiancé cleared his throat. ''I know you're angry with me. No bride wants to hear her prospective bridegroom is having second thoughts. Although I would think you would appreciate my honesty.''

Haley frowned. Allan was saying almost the same thing her father had. It was creepy.

''I do appreciate your honesty,'' she said. ''As I hope you'll appreciate mine. Being away had allowed me to think about my life, what I want and what I don't want. I don't want to be engaged to you anymore.''

''Haley, you're not being reasonable. Of course

you want to punish me, but don't you think you're taking this a little too far?"

She could hear the temper in his voice. "I'm not trying to do anything but tell you our relationship is over."

"Where are you?"

"Why does that matter?"

"Because you don't know what you're saying. Tell me where you are and I'll come get you and take you home. I made a mistake and I'm sorry. You need to forgive me so we can go on with our lives."

"Why won't you listen to me? There is no 'us,' no 'we.'"

"But you love me. We belong together."

She held the phone out in front of her and stared at it. Was there some kind of technical malfunction that prevented her words from getting through?

"I don't love you," she said slowly and clearly. "I don't believe you love me."

"We have a wedding in less than two weeks. Are you telling me you want to break things off now?"

"Yes, I am." She closed her eyes. "Allan, we both got caught up in what other people thought. I'm not sure we ever saw each other for who we are. I accept my share of the blame for that. I never did a good job of going against other's expectations. But that's changing. I want my life back. I want to make my own choices. I want to be in love the way my parents were and I know I could never love you like that. I'm sorry. I hope you can find someone to make you really happy."

She opened her eyes and hung up the phone. As she turned, she saw Kevin standing in the doorway.

He shrugged when she looked at him. "My mom had to go to the grocery store, so she dropped me off first." His dark eyes softened with concern. "Allan?"

She nodded.

"You okay?"

She nodded again, but she was lying. Talking to her ex-fiancé had shaken her and the only place she wanted to be was in Kevin's arms.

"How did your parents love each other?" he asked.

"With their whole hearts. My father never remarried because he couldn't find someone else to love as much and anything less wasn't worth having. I don't think Allan understands that we never cared about each other. I shouldn't have let myself be swayed by what other people think. I shouldn't have ever dated him, let alone gotten engaged."

"You figured it out in time."

She nodded. "So, how was your morning?"

"Better than yours. Gage and I talked about the next step. We're going to California in a few weeks to find the rest of the Haynes clan. It turns out there are several other brothers."

He looked both happy and nervous about the prospect. Haley wasn't sure who moved first, but suddenly he was holding her and she was hugging him as hard as she could. Everything might be spinning out of control but with Kevin nearby she felt as if she could withstand even a tornado.

"It's all right," he murmured, kissing her cheek, then her nose.

She tried to smile but couldn't. "I wish we were still on the road," she told him. "I wish it was just the two of us and that we never had to come back to the real world."

"I wish that, too."

Her heart swelled. "Really."

He nodded.

The phone rang. He gave her a quick kiss on the mouth, then reached past her to grab it. "Hello?"

Haley walked to the cupboard for a glass, but an odd premonition made her turn around. Kevin stood listening. His face was unreadable but she knew something was wrong.

"Yes, this is the Harmon residence," he said coolly. "Yes. She's here."

He covered the mouthpiece with his hand and looked at her. "It's Allan."

She shouldn't have been surprised. The church had a Caller-ID system installed a couple of years ago. Allan simply had to walk into the front office and check to see where she'd called from. Obviously Vivian and Howard didn't have their calls blocked.

She moved next to Kevin and took the phone from him. "There's no point to this, Allan," she said.

"You're making a mistake and we both know it," he said. "I've looked up the address for this number. I'll be there in the morning to pick you up. Try to be mature this time, Haley. It wouldn't look good for you to run away again."

She felt cold and angry. "That's what matters, isn't it? How things look, not how they are. I'm not going back with you."

"Of course you are, but we'll discuss it when I get there. By the way, who are these people you're staying with? You aren't alone with a man are you?"

She hung up the phone without saying anything else. Kevin watched her. "He's coming for you."

He made the sentence a statement, not a question. Haley nodded slowly. "He said he would be here in the morning. I guess he'll fly into Dallas and drive the rest of the way."

"What do you want to do? If you need to go, I'll understand."

His gaze was steady. She saw understanding in his eyes. He wouldn't judge her for running. He knew how precious her freedom was.

But she wasn't the same person she'd been a couple of weeks ago. She'd changed, maybe she'd grown up.

"I'm staying," she told him. "I'm a fighter. I think I always have been, I just never bothered to stand up for myself before."

"I won't let him hurt you."

Haley smiled. How had she ever gotten so lucky as to find Kevin? "I know you won't."

He held out his arms and she stepped into his embrace. This was where she belonged. But how long would she be allowed to stay?

Chapter Thirteen

While Howard and Vivian went to bed shortly before ten, Haley and Kevin stayed up to finish the movie they were watching. At least, Kevin was watching it. Haley couldn't concentrate. Not when she was worried about Allan showing up in the morning. While she didn't doubt her resolve to do as she wanted and not as he insisted, she was fighting against twenty-five years of doing what everyone else thought was best for her. What if she wasn't strong enough to stand up to him?

Kevin reached for the remote and clicked off the television. "You don't need to be worried," he told her.

She smiled at him. "Thanks for the vote of confidence. I just wish I had a little more experience standing up to people and telling them no."

"Are you concerned about your feelings for Allan?"

He asked the question casually, as if the answer didn't matter. Haley hoped that was an act and not the truth. "No. Whatever I felt for Allan, it was never love and it died a long time ago. It's the whole expectation thing."

"Just say no."

She laughed. "I'll do my best."

"We can practice tonight."

"I don't want to say no to you."

She'd spoken the words without thinking but as soon as she said them, she realized how true they were. She never wanted to say no to Kevin. She only wanted to say yes. Yes, she loved him. Yes, she wanted to be with him always. Yes, he was her heart's desire.

Of course. Why hadn't she figured this out before? She'd been falling in love with him from the first night they'd met. He was everything she could ever want in a man. She could imagine being with him for the rest of her life. Knowing that there would only be him made her want them both to live forever.

"Haley, what's wrong?"

She turned to look at him. His face had grown familiar to her. She knew his voice, his smile, his sense of humor. She admired his need to do the right thing. She trusted him. She wanted him.

"Make love with me," she whispered.

He stared at her. "Haley, we've been over this before."

She shook her head. "I'm sure. I'm more sure than

I've ever been about anything. I want you to be my first.'' *My only*. But she didn't say that. She wouldn't play love like a card in a game. This was too important.

She watched the desire ignite in his eyes, but there was caution, as well.

''I don't want you to have regrets,'' he said.

How like him, she thought happily. To want her to be sure. ''If you don't want me, I won't ask again.'' She took his hands in hers. ''The only regret I'm going to have is if we don't make love. I know I'll spend the rest of my life being sorry.''

He stared at her for a long time. She didn't move because as much as he needed her to be sure, she needed the same thing.

Silence stretched until it nearly snapped. Haley stopped breathing. Finally, when she was sure he was going to tell her no, he leaned forward and brushed her mouth with his.

''There aren't any words to tell you how much I want you,'' he said. ''But not here, on the sofa. I want to make love with you in bed.'' He smiled. ''At least my folks sleep downstairs. We don't have to worry about them.''

She wasn't worried about anything. When he rose and held out his hand, she placed her fingers on his palm. They made the short walk to his bedroom at the far end of the house.

As she entered, Haley had a brief impression of light blue walls and shelves filled with mementos from a busy childhood. There were baseballs and sports posters, part of an engine on a desk and a stack of books. A dark blue comforter covered the full-size bed. Kevin walked to the nightstand and clicked on the lamp, then returned to stand in front of her. He cupped her face in his hands and studied her.

"I thought you were pretty the first time I saw you," he said. "But I was wrong. You're beautiful."

His compliment both pleased and embarrassed her. "I'm not so special."

"You are." His dark eyes glowed with intensity. "You're sweet and funny and smart. You care about other people, yet you're willing to stand up for what you think is right."

Her heart beat faster with every word. Knowing that Kevin cared about her, that he thought she was more than ordinary, made her want to burst free of the room and soar toward the heavens. Then he bent his head and pressed his mouth to hers. As the heat of his kiss spiraled through her body, she decided that staying right here on solid ground might be a better plan.

They'd kissed enough times that the contact was familiar. Soft, tempting brushes of sensitive skin against sensitive skin. As her arms came around to hold him close, her lips parted to admit him. He swept inside, touching her tongue with his, making her blood race and her body heat. Her breasts swelled and a sweet pressure built low in her belly.

He aroused her. With just a kiss, and sometimes with just a look. Knowing they were going to really make love sent a tingling sensation through her midsection. She wasn't afraid. Not with Kevin. He'd never done anything but make her world a perfect place to be. Tonight would be no different.

As he deepened the kiss, he rubbed his hands up and down her back. When he cupped her rear, she instinctively arched toward him. Her stomach brushed against him and she felt that he was already hard.

He wanted her. He'd said as much, but the physical proof delighted her. She remembered the last time they'd been together, when she'd seen him naked and touched him until he'd experienced the same release she had. She wanted that again, only this time she wanted him inside her. She wanted them to be one.

She felt his fingers on the back zipper of the summer dress she'd slipped on for dinner. As he pulled the tab, warm air brushed against her bare skin. She pulled back enough to drop her arms to her sides and shimmy out of the dress. At the same time, she kicked off her sandals. Kevin pulled off his shoes and socks, then shrugged out of his shirt. He moved to the bed and sat on the edge. Wearing only a bra and panties, she slipped between his parted legs.

With him sitting and her standing, she was taller. She bent her head and kissed him. He rested his hands on her bare waist. She could feel the imprint of each finger. He was warm and strong and, even undressed, she felt safe.

His hands moved higher. She braced herself for the first sweep of his hands on her breasts. Her breath caught in anticipation, then she sighed her pleasure as he cupped her curves. Even through the fabric of her bra, she felt his gentle caress. When his thumbs brushed over her tight nipples, she gasped as fire blazed through her.

She fumbled for the hooks of her bra and tugged it off. When the garment fell to the ground, Kevin looked at her bare chest. His breath caught audibly, which made her thighs tremble with excitement.

"So perfect," he murmured before leaning close and taking her left nipple in his mouth.

Gentle sucking sent ribbons of need curling through her. Between her legs, her body swelled and dampened in anticipation. His fingers teased her right breast, mimicking what he was doing with his tongue. It felt so right, so amazing. She could barely stand. Her head fell back and she wanted to surrender right this minute. Kevin could take her any way he wanted. As long as he touched her like that, as long as the tension built and the pleasure grew, she was his to command.

He moved his mouth to her right breast. More. She wanted more. She wanted this moment to never end. She wanted—

A single finger stroked her between her thighs. The unexpected touch chased away her last coherent thought. Breathing was impossible. She could only feel the light, teasing whisper of movement. It wasn't enough. She tried to part her legs, but she was standing between his and there wasn't room. She clutched at him, pulling him closer, wanting, needing bare skin against bare skin.

He straightened and tugged at her panties. The air tingled against her damp nipple. There were so many sensations. His hands against her legs, the sheets when he pulled back the comforter and eased her onto the bed. The sound of the zipper on his jeans being pulled downward seemed loud in the night.

She wasn't afraid. Not even a little. All of this felt right. This was the man she was meant to love. There would only ever be him, so how could joining with him be anything but her destiny?

He pulled off the rest of his clothing with one quick movement. She had a brief glimpse of his heavy arousal, then he knelt between her legs and bent low to kiss her right knee.

The swept of his tongue tickled. She giggled softly.

"So you're ticklish," he said, raising his head and looking at her.

She nodded. "Pretty much everywhere."

"I know one place you're not."

"I'm not sure there is one. I remember—"

Whatever she'd been planning to say was lost when he bent low and pressed an openmouthed kiss on the top of her thigh. She would have sworn she was ticklish there, too, but the intimate contact surprised her so much she couldn't react. Just as well, because his next move was to reach between her legs and gently part her, exposing her most intimate self to his gaze.

She barely had time to register shock when he kissed her *there*. Right there. Just like that. With his lips and his tongue and—

The pleasure slammed into her. It ripped through her, sucking away air and the ability to move. She could only feel the stroke of his tongue, the gentle circling, the heat, the need. Every muscle tensed harder and tighter. Her body ached and burned. He moved slowly, deliberately, setting a pace that made her hips pulse in time with each flick of paradise.

The wanting crested, then went higher and higher until it was impossible to reach so far and still want more. Tiny spasms rippled through her fingers. She pulled her knees back and gasped, then found herself reaching again and again. There was a single heartbeat during which she balanced on the edge of the universe before the sweep of his tongue sent an explosion of intense pleasure flying through every cell in her body.

It was like coming apart, while staying together. The climax shook her down to her soul and left her gasping. Nothing, not even what they'd done before, had prepared her for the intensity that seemed to go on forever before finally fading into aftershocks.

Kevin moved next to her and pulled her into his arms. She clung to him until she could think again, until the world stopped spinning. When she was finally back, she felt his soft kisses on her face.

"Wow," she said, opening her eyes and trying not to grin too broadly. "That was really great."

"I'm glad you liked it."

"No, it was really amazing."

He smiled. "I guess you'd been saving up for a while."

"Too long."

She thought about asking him to do that again when she felt the brush of something hard and insistent on her thigh. She reached between them and closed her fingers around his arousal.

"Can I do that to you?"

His expression turned rueful. "Sure. It would take all of thirty seconds."

She considered her options. "Maybe later," she said. "I want us to make love the traditional way."

His expression tightened. "Haley, we don't have to—"

She pressed a finger to his mouth. "I want to. I want you inside of me. I want to know how that feels and I want you to be my first time." She cleared her throat. "In case you're worried, there isn't any, you know, *physical* proof that I'm a virgin. My doctor told me that a while ago."

One corner of his mouth turned up. "Good. Then it won't hurt."

She didn't expect it to. Not with Kevin.

He pushed on her hip until she rolled onto her back. He propped his hand on one of her hands and rested the other on her stomach.

"You understand what happens when couples make love," he said.

She wasn't sure if he was asking a question or not, so she nodded anyway. "You, ah, are inside of me."

"Right." He slid his hand between her legs. "This is where I was touching you before."

He rubbed his fingertips against her swollen center. Instantly her toes curled.

"It was very nice," she said, barely able to speak as he continued to touch that one amazing spot.

"This is where I go inside."

He slipped a finger into her, all the while keeping his thumb moving back and forth.

The combination of sensations caught her off

guard. Finger and thumb moved together. The wanting began, as did the tension. He bent low and licked her breasts. It was a pretty unbeatable combination, she thought as her eyes fluttered closed. Why hadn't anyone told her she could feel this good?

He slipped out of her, then moved back inside, but this time there was more pressure. Two fingers, maybe? She liked how the stroking brushed the sides. As he pushed in, he reached up and she groaned as her body contracted in delight. He began to move faster. His lips closed over her nipple and he sucked, taking the tight point into his mouth. It was too much. It was everything. Tension built. She could feel it. She was getting closer and closer. She was right there. She was—

He stopped. Haley opened her eyes.

Kevin shrugged. "Sorry. We have a logistical issue."

He rolled away and opened a drawer in his nightstand. She caught a glimpse of a small box, then realized he'd reached for a condom.

But she was on the Pill. Her brain clicked into gear. Oh. There was more to worry about than just getting pregnant. Even humming with unreleased need, she appreciated that he was trying to protect her. The tender gesture made her eyes burn.

He pulled on the protection then knelt between her legs.

"Where were we?" he asked with a smile as he found her center with his fingers and began to rub.

In less than fifteen seconds, she was right back on the edge. Her breathing came in short pants and she arched her back as her release approached. Then she felt something thick and hard pressing into her. It was bigger than two fingers.

He moved slowly, filling her. Her body stretched to accommodate the unfamiliar presence. Some of her tension faded, but he kept moving his fingers and she soon found herself reaching for her release. Then he began to move.

This was it! Haley couldn't believe they were actually doing it. She opened her eyes and saw Kevin watching her.

"You all right?" he asked. His voice sounded low and hoarse.

She nodded, then raised herself up on one elbow. He was kneeling close to her. She could see him entering her and pulling out. The hand against her center continued to rub her. She could see and feel him touching her at the same time. It was the most incredible experience ever.

The slow, steady in and out became less unfamiliar. Then it started to feel kind of nice. Suddenly the combination of his fingers and his...well, you know, were too much. She fell back on the bed and closed her eyes. Need grew. Her body tensed.

He shifted and then he was on top of her, holding her close, kissing her. She wrapped her arms around him, savoring the weight of his body and how they were really joined together. It was everything she'd ever wanted.

He started to move a little faster. Suddenly she was aware that the tension hadn't faded. If anything it seemed to be building. In and out, in and out. She clutched at his hips. More, she thought frantically.

Somehow he knew. He read her mind, or maybe it was her nails digging into his rear. Whatever the cause, he filled her again and again until something inside her snapped and she lost herself in a release unlike the others she'd experienced. Even as she climaxed, she seemed to be building and releasing at the same time until there was nothing but the feel of him inside of her and the rush of pleasure.

Kevin felt the first spasm deep inside Haley. She'd been so close before that he'd hoped he could take her over the edge, but he hadn't been sure. He felt the powerful contractions that ripped through her. She clung to him, writhing, gasping, calling out his name. Her legs wrapped around his hips as she opened herself even wider.

He'd been holding back but now he plunged into her harder and harder. The dull ache in his leg didn't diminish the building pressure. Pressure that threatened his ability to hold back. He sucked in his breath, holding on until her contractions exploded into one long powerful convulsion that destroyed his last shred of control. He lost himself in her, as his body shuddered with release.

When he could breathe again, he opened his eyes and looked at her. Haley's expression was one of blissful contentment. She smiled.

''You're really good at that,'' she murmured.

''Not bad for our first time together.''

She nodded.

Her cheeks were flushed, as was her chest. Her hair

was mussed and her lips were swollen. She looked like a woman who had been thoroughly pleasured. She looked like a woman in love.

Wishful thinking, he told himself. With his defenses down, he could no longer ignore the obvious. That he'd fallen for her. He didn't know when it had happened. Maybe that first night when she offered to be forbidden fruit. Or had it been later, when she'd charmed him and made him believe that he wasn't always a screwup? Regardless, he loved her now.

"Thank you, Kevin," she said, and kissed him. "I'll remember this night forever."

He thought of how empty his world was going to be when she was gone. "I'll remember it just as long," he promised. "No matter what."

Haley tried to hold on to the glow as long as possible, but by noon, it had faded. She kept glancing at the clock, then wishing she hadn't.

Kevin sat across from her at the kitchen table. Vivian and Howard were both at work, so they had the house to themselves. She was glad. She didn't want Kevin's parents to witness whatever was going to happen.

"Do you know what you're going to say?" Kevin asked.

"No. I'm going to try to be mature and not to call him names."

"He probably deserves them."

She tried to smile. "I wish I'd practiced my swearing more."

He took her hand and squeezed. "You never swore

at all. Do you want me to hang around or would you rather be alone with him?''

Her breath caught. ''Don't go. Please. If you can stand to stay, I would really appreciate you being here.''

''I'm not going anywhere.''

His dark eyes promised. She studied his handsome face, the wave in his black hair, the way his shoulders seemed so broad. Her heart ached with her love for him. Last night had been the most wonderful experience of her life, and all because of him.

Impulsively she rose to her feet and crossed to his chair. He shifted back so she could settle on his lap. He wrapped his arms around her as she clung to him. If only he would never let her go.

''I'm not going to say anything,'' he told her, ''but if he uses physical force, I'm going to beat the crap out of him.''

Despite her apprehension, she laughed. ''Allan isn't the physical-force type.''

''Can I beat him up anyway?''

She looked at him. ''You'd do that for me?''

''Sure.''

''No one has ever offered to beat someone up for me before.''

''I'm a rough, tough kinda guy.''

He was that and so much more. He was—

A car pulled up in front of the house. Haley stiffened, then slid to her feet. ''He's here.''

She walked toward the front door. Kevin followed partway and stopped in the hallway. She thought about asking him to stand next to her, then changed her mind. This was her problem and she would solve it herself. Knowing Kevin was close gave her strength.

She waited for the knock before opening the door. Allan stood on the wide porch. She blinked in surprise as she took in his close-cropped blond hair and light eyes. In her mind, he'd always been fairly good-looking, but now he seemed pale and cold.

"Hello, Allan," she said, stepping back to allow him into the house.

"What is this place?" he asked by way of greeting. "Whose house is this? How do you know these people?"

"They're friends."

He looked around the living room, then turned his attention to her. "Are you packed?"

"No."

He frowned. "You're going to make this difficult, aren't you?"

"If by difficult you mean I'm not going to do what you tell me, then yes. I already explained everything on the phone. I told you not to come. There was a reason for that. I'm not coming back with you."

His gaze narrowed. "You cut your hair."

The statement sounded more like an accusation. Haley reached up and fingered the shorn locks. She'd nearly forgotten about her hair-based rebellion the first day she left. In the time she'd been gone, she'd gotten used to short hair.

"I like it this way," she said.

"At least it will grow back." He reached for her

wrist. ''Show me your room. We'll pack your things and get out of here.''

Haley shook free of his grip and stepped back. She looked at the man she'd dated for nearly five years. His eyes were too close together and his expression was pinched. Why hadn't she noticed that before? He never listened to her. They'd never done anything she wanted. Their relationship had never been a partnership—instead Allan had been in charge and she had done his bidding.

She closed her eyes and tried to picture Allan naked, touching her, making love with her. Her imagination wasn't up to the task. She didn't want his hands on her body. She didn't want anything to do with him.

''I don't love you, Allan,'' she said firmly. ''I'm not sure I even like you. You want a woman to do what you say, and I want a man who is interested in my opinions. You want to be in charge, I want a partner.''

''You don't know what you want.''

''Yes, I do. I want to love someone the way my father loved my mother. I want to love with a deep honesty that touches my soul. I want to be a teacher and go to Hawaii on my honeymoon. I want to have children right away. I want a big old house that looks lived in, not designer perfect. I want a man who believes in me, and who I can believe in. I don't want you, Allan. I don't want to marry you, and I don't want anything to do with you.''

He flushed. ''You don't know what you're saying. Your father wants this marriage.''

"Maybe he wanted it once, when he thought I loved you, but as soon as I tell him the truth, he'll back me up." She sighed. "Let me go. You don't really love me. You haven't for a long time. In fact you were the one questioning whether or not we should get married. Obviously something inside you told you it was wrong."

"Last-minute jitters," he told her. "Nothing more."

She moved close to him. "Tell me you love me with all your heart. Tell me you didn't feel even a little relief when I ran away."

"Haley, you're—" He broke off. His mouth twisted. "You're on drugs."

She burst out laughing. "It has to be that, right? Because I couldn't possibly have figured out how to be my own person."

He glared at her. "If you don't come back with me right this minute, it's over between us."

She walked to the door. "Goodbye, Allan. I hope you find someone to make you happy."

He stalked toward her. "You'll regret this. I won't take you back."

"You shouldn't. I'm the wrong woman for you."

He stepped onto the porch, then swung to face her. "You're disappointing a lot of people with your behavior."

Magic words designed to make her feel small. She ignored the automatic guilt. "Those who care about me will understand and support my decision. Those who don't will judge me. I can live with that."

"You're making a mistake."

She watched him walk to his rental car. He paused before climbing inside. ''This is your last chance.''

He waited and when she didn't say anything, he got inside and drove away. Haley watched him go and felt only relief.

Chapter Fourteen

Kevin listened to the sound of the front door closing. Haley had done it—she'd stood up to Allan and reclaimed her life. She'd come a long way from the young woman who had walked into a bar, looking for trouble. While he'd never doubted her ability to do whatever she wanted, he knew she'd been afraid. Until recently, she'd always let others' opinions dictate her actions. That wasn't likely to happen again.

"Did you hear?" Haley called as she burst into the hallway where he leaned against the wall. "Wasn't that something? I couldn't believe he expected me to come back with him. I mean, I told him and told him I wouldn't. Why on earth did I go out with him? I was crazy."

"You were doing what your family wanted."

She considered that. "By family you mean everyone at church.'' She sighed. ''You're right. They seemed so happy to see me with Allan and I didn't care. I wasn't crazy about him, but he wasn't too awful. I guess over time I thought I was in love with him because that seemed to be the next logical step. Just think, if he hadn't had second thoughts, I might never have run away. I could have ended up married to him.''

Kevin walked into the kitchen, with Haley on his heels. ''You wouldn't have gone through with it.''

He took a seat at the table. She plopped down next to him. ''I hope you're right. I want to think that I would have balked at the last second, but I'll never know for sure.'' She shook her head. ''I couldn't believe he accused me of being on drugs. Oh, like that's the only possible explanation for me turning him down. What a creep.''

''You didn't even let me beat him up.''

She leaned toward him and rested her hand on his arms. ''I love that you offered to do that for me. It was so sweet.''

Her face was bright with happiness. Humor flashed in her eyes. She looked young and alive, and filled with possibilities. There was a whole world waiting for her out there. One she'd never experienced. Haley had dreams.

He knew then what he'd always known but had never wanted to admit out loud. That she deserved to be free to find whatever her heart desired. He loved her too much to tie her down when she'd just found her freedom.

He cupped her face. ''You did good today. You

proved something to Allan, but more importantly, you proved something to yourself. No matter what happens, you'll always remember that you have the strength and determination to do whatever you want. You spread your wings.''

She smiled. ''I like that analogy.''

''It's time to take them out for a test drive.''

Her smile faded. ''Kevin?''

He could still remember the way the bullet had slammed into his leg. The pain had come as a surprise. This time he was expecting it, but the intensity still stunned him. It was as if he was being ripped apart from the inside.

He swallowed. ''You need to go live your life. It's all out there. Everything you could ever want.''

''But what if everything I want is right here?'' She blinked several times and her lips trembled. ''Do you want me to leave?''

''This is about you.''

Tears filled her eyes. ''I understand what you're saying and I even know why, but I want to stay.''

He wanted that, too. More than he'd wanted anything. For the first time in his life, he'd finally found a woman he could love forever. Unfortunately she was the one woman he couldn't be with. Fate sure had a twisted sense of humor.

''I'm heading back to Washington. I have a job waiting there.''

''And the promotion?'' she asked.

He shrugged. ''If they still want me.''

''For real?''

He kissed her. "Because of you, Haley. I'm willing to take the chance. You have to do the same."

Tears spilled down her cheeks. "I love you. I want to marry you."

He felt that blow down to his soul. "I love you, too. I want…" He wanted so many things. "I want what's right. I told you from the beginning I wasn't going to screw up with you and I meant it."

He brushed away her tears. "All your life people have told you what to do and you've listened. I'm not going to be like them. I want us to be together, but not like this. You need time to figure out what's right for you, to find your own life. Once that's straight, you come find me. I'll be waiting."

She bit back a sob. "F-for how long?"

"For always. You're the first woman I've ever loved. What I felt before doesn't begin to compare. There's just you, Haley. I'll be waiting."

Telling herself that Kevin was right and actually leaving were two different things. Haley had to pull over twice in the first twenty miles because she was crying too hard to see the road. She loved him and he loved her, so why was she leaving?

She brushed away the moisture and checked her mirrors before easing back into traffic. The answer was simple. She was leaving because as much as she loved him, she needed time to think things through. She'd fallen for him so fast that she could barely keep up. She needed to calm down and to take a look at her life. She needed to go home, to make peace with her father and to reevaluate her world.

The childish part of her demanded that she turn around and drive back to Possum Landing. She loved Kevin; she wanted to be with him right now. But the sensible part of her knew that getting closure was more important.

She reached into her shirt pocket and felt the card he'd given her. On it was his home number, his work number and his pager number. When she was ready, she was to call. But until then, they would be apart.

He wanted her to be sure. She suspected he had considered the possibility that this was just a vacation fling for her. That time and distance would cause a change in heart.

"I'm my father's daughter," she whispered as she drove. "He's loved the same woman all his life. You'd better be waiting, because I'll be coming to find you."

Haley walked into the church office late the following afternoon. Her trip home had been much faster than her aborted journey to Hawaii. She'd ignored all the tempting roadside shops and museums, instead driving until she was exhausted, then getting a room for a few hours before continuing north.

She looked around at the familiar office with its big windows and glass-enclosed bookcases. Marie's desk sat in the center of the room. Her chair was empty, but Haley could hear her talking in the other room.

In some ways Haley felt as if she'd been gone a lifetime. In other ways it seemed she'd only left a few minutes before. So much had changed and yet so much remained the same.

The door to her father's office opened. Marie stepped out, saw her and screamed.

"Haley! It's Haley!"

The petite fifty-something brunette rushed forward. Papers went flying as she wrapped her arms around Haley in a bear hug strong enough to snap ribs.

"We were so worried. You should have called more. You look fine. Are you all right? Allan came back and said some horrible things. He and your father had words. I tried not to listen, but I couldn't help it. Now Allan is going to be looking for another position. Oh, and you cut your hair!"

Marie paused for breath. Haley hugged her back, then kissed her cheek.

"I missed you, too," she said. "I'm sorry I worried you."

She didn't know what to think about her father and Allan, but she would find out what had happened soon enough.

"Hello, Haley."

She looked up and saw her father standing in the doorway. He was tall and as handsome as ever. When he smiled at her, she felt all her concerns fade. Whatever she'd done, he still loved her, would always love her. Of course, she thought as she hurried to his side. Why had she been so afraid to tell him what she was feeling?

"Oh, Daddy."

She hugged him close, feeling the familiar combination of strength and love radiating from him. He pulled her into his office and shut the door, then rested his hands on her shoulders and studied her.

"It seems you survived your adventure," he said, his low voice rumbling in the small room.

She nodded. "I did just fine. I'm all grown up now."

"You've been that for a while, although no one around here noticed. Not even me." He sighed. "Things have been very interesting since Allan returned from Texas. Why don't you tell me your version of things?"

He motioned to one of the leather chairs in front of his desk, then settled himself in the other.

She didn't know where to begin. "What did Allan say about me?"

"That you'd cut your hair and were probably on drugs." Her father sighed. "It was his only explanation for your refusal to come back and marry him."

"What did you think?"

"That you didn't love him. Was I right?"

She nodded. "I didn't realize it for a long time. I knew something was wrong, but I couldn't figure out what. When he said he was having second thoughts, I got so angry. I felt that I'd given up everything I wanted to make him happy and then *he* had second thoughts? It was so unfair. That's why I took off. I couldn't stand it anymore."

"I pushed you into a relationship with him," her father said. When she started to protest, he cut her off with a wave. "We both know it, Haley. You've always been so eager to please and do the right thing. I convinced myself you were in love with him, but I think deep in my heart I knew you were with Allan because I wanted it and the congregation wanted it. I'm sorry. I should have seen what was happening and told you not to get married unless you were absolutely sure you were in love with him.''

"Thank you, Daddy," she whispered.

She'd only been gone for a short time, yet her father seemed to have changed. There was more gray in his dark blond hair, or maybe she'd just never noticed it before. He was a good man. Wise and kind and giving. But every memory she had was of him by himself.

"Mom would never have wanted you to live so alone," she said.

He raised his eyebrows. "What brought that on?"

"I don't know, but it's true. She's been gone twenty-five years. Wasn't there even one woman who touched your heart?"

"Maybe." He shrugged. "I loved her so much. Losing her was the worst thing that ever happened to me. I didn't want to risk that again. Besides, I wasn't lonely. I had you, my work. Friends. God."

"During the day, but what about at night?"

"God is with us always."

She smiled. "You know what I mean."

"I do. I've thought about it from time to time."

"Is there someone?"

His gaze narrowed. "We're supposed to be talking about you, young lady."

She laughed. "All right. Keep your secrets. But if there's a spark, I think you should pursue it." She twisted her fingers together. "I know what you meant when you used to talk to me about loving Mom."

"You've found someone?"

She nodded. She could feel the smile curving her lips and wouldn't have been surprised if her entire body started to glow. "His name is Kevin and he's a U.S. Marshal. He's so wonderful, Daddy. He's strong and caring and generous. He loves me and wants only the best for me. He's a good man."

"So where is this paragon of virtue? As your father, it's my duty to terrify him into taking good care of you."

She laughed. "That won't be necessary. He already does." Her humor faded. "He's in Texas and will soon be flying to Washington, D.C. That's where he works. That's where I want to be."

Her father frowned. "What's standing in your way? Is he married?"

"Oh, Daddy. He's not married. He wants me to be sure." How exactly was she supposed to explain the complexity of her relationship with Kevin? Did her father really want to know she'd spent their entire time together trying to get him to sleep with her? She thought not.

"He knows about Allan and how I've been doing what everyone wanted me to do and not what I wanted. He loves me and wants me to come back to him, but first he wants me to figure out what I want. He says I need to be doing for myself now."

Her father winced. "I didn't mean not to listen."

"I know. It just sort of happened. I was willing to

do what everyone thought was right. I should have stood up to people, but I didn't know how."

"Do you now?"

"Yes. I love you, Daddy, but I'm not going to be able to live here anymore. I want to be a school-teacher. I want to marry Kevin and have a life with him."

"It sounds to me as if you've got everything planned."

"Pretty much."

"Then what are you doing here? I thought you said your young man was in Washington."

Haley caught her breath. Her father's love and acceptance filled her heart with a joy and peace that nearly gave her wings. She threw herself at him.

"I love you, Daddy."

He hugged her tightly. "I love you, too. I always have. You're a wonderful daughter and one of the most special people it has been my privilege to know. God blessed me when he brought you into my life. But it seems to me, it's long past time for you to be moving on. Just don't forget your old man in all the excitement of your new life."

"I won't," she promised. "Not ever."

Kevin glanced at the clock and tried not to do the math. Unfortunately his brain supplied him with the information. Ten days, seven hours. That's how long it had been since Haley had left Possum Landing. He hadn't heard from her since.

They'd made a deal, he reminded himself. She

would go back to her old life and decide what she wanted. If it was him, she would be in touch, if not…

He didn't want to think about that. He didn't want to think about a cold, empty life spent missing her. He'd done the right thing by letting her go, he only wished it didn't have to hurt so badly.

While he knew he wouldn't get over her, he figured the loneliness would get easier in time. He'd accepted the promotion and was now swamped with several field projects he had to coordinate. He had his own office, an assistant and a team reporting directly to him. The pay increase meant that should Haley return they would be able to afford to get a house right off. And if she didn't…he'd have a hell of a nest egg.

In the meantime, he kept busy with his new responsibilities and planning his upcoming trip to California. He and Gage had decided to e-mail their long-lost relatives. They'd found the Haynes brothers to be excited by the thought of new relatives. The date had been set for the big family reunion. Kevin's brother, Nash, was going to meet them there, and Gage was trying to get in touch with his brother, Quinn.

Everything was coming together—except for wanting Haley back.

Just his dumb luck, he thought grimly. He'd finally fallen in love with someone he'd had to let go. Nothing in life was easy, right?

The intercom buzzed. Kevin hit the button. "Yes?"

"You have a visitor. May I send her in?"

Her? Haley? He told himself it wasn't possible, that

it was too soon, that she might not still be in love with him... But he didn't want to believe it.

"Sure," he said, telling himself he had to get over expecting her to walk through the door. He stood and waited.

Either his mind was playing tricks on him or the world has stopped turning because twenty seconds later a pretty young woman with hazel-blue eyes and a wide, winning smile stepped into his office. She wore a short denim skirt and a cropped T-shirt that exposed a sliver of stomach and sent need racing south.

Haley closed the door behind her. "You said to go get my life in order. That took about fifteen minutes. I didn't think you'd believe me if I rushed right back, and I thought you had a good point. So I talked to my dad, I made lists, I tried to get over you." She shrugged. "I can't. I love you. So how long do I have to wait until we can be together?"

He didn't remember moving, but suddenly she was in his arms. He kissed her, tasting her, needing her. Loving her.

All the pain of being alone, of missing her, faded. She loved him. She still loved him.

"I love you. I've missed you," he murmured, kissing her cheeks, her mouth, her chin, her nose. "Every damn day has been hell."

She looked at him and smiled. "Compound swearing. I'm so impressed." She touched his face. "I missed you, too. With every breath. I love you, Kevin. How could I not? You wanted what was right for me, even when it hurt you. Isn't that the real definition of love? Wanting what's right for the other person regardless of your own needs? The thing is, *you're* right for me. I know you're not perfect, but that's okay. I'm not perfect, either. And you're the best man I've ever known. I love you so much and I'm proud to be loved by you. I want to be with you always. I want to marry you and go to California and meet your family. I want to make a home with you and have children with you. I want to grow old with you and hold hands and make love until we're old and gray and should probably know better. But we'll do it anyway because we can't resist each other.''

She paused. "But I'll wait if you want me to."

He laughed and swung her around the room. "I don't want to wait even a day." When he set her on her feet, he stared into her eyes. "You've said all the fancy words, so I only have those left in my heart. Marry me, Haley. I will do my best to make you happy. I will keep you safe, honor you, love you."

"Yes." She kissed him. "Yes. Of course."

He angled his head and deepened the kiss. Passion exploded between them. It would always be like this, he realized. He would always want her and she would always be there for him. He could see their future as clearly as if it were a movie up on the wall, and it made him humble with gratitude.

"There's just one thing," she said, pulling back. "We have to go to Ohio because my dad wants to meet you and I sort of said we could be married there. Is that okay?"

"Absolutely. As long as Allan isn't performing the ceremony."

She giggled. "Nope. He's long gone."

"Then Ohio it is. And then Hawaii, for our honeymoon."

"Well, I've been thinking about that. Let's get married and then go to California to meet your family. We can do Hawaii next year."

"I thought that's what had started everything. You were driving to Hawaii."

"It was, until I realized that I'd found my own private paradise with you. It's not about the location. It's about being with the man I love and having him love me back."

"I do," he vowed.

"Forever?"

"Longer."

* * * * *

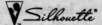

SPECIAL EDITION™

Continues the captivating series
from *USA TODAY* bestselling author

SUSAN MALLERY

These heart-stoppin' hunks are rugged,
ready and able to steal your heart!

Don't miss the next irresistible books in the series...

COMPLETELY SMITTEN
On sale February 2003
(SE #1520)

ONE IN A MILLION
On sale June 2003
(SE #1543)

Available at your favorite retail outlet.

Where love comes alive™

Visit Silhouette at www.eHarlequin.com   SSEHH

Don't miss the latest miniseries from award-winning author Marie Ferrarella:

Meet...

Sherry Campbell—ambitious newswoman who makes headlines when a handsome billionaire arrives to sweep her off her feet...and shepherd her new son into the world!
A BILLIONAIRE AND A BABY, SE#1528,
available March 2003

Joanna Prescott—Nine months after her visit to the sperm bank, her old love rescues her from a burning house—then delivers her baby....
A BACHELOR AND A BABY, SD#1503,
available April 2003

Chris "C.J." Jones—FBI agent, expectant mother and always on the case. When the baby comes, will her irresistible partner be by her side?
THE BABY MISSION, IM#1220, available May 2003

Lori O'Neill—A forbidden attraction blows down this pregnant Lamaze teacher's tough-woman facade and makes her consider the love of a lifetime!
BEAUTY AND THE BABY, SR#1668,
available June 2003

The Mom Squad—these single mothers-to-be are ready for labor...and true love!

Where love comes alive™

Visit Silhouette at www.eHarlequin.com   SXSTMS

USA TODAY bestselling author

LINDSAY McKENNA

**brings you a brand-new series
featuring Morgan Trayhern and his team!**

WOMAN OF INNOCENCE
(Silhouette Special Edition #1442)

An innocent beauty longing for adventure. A rugged mercenary
sworn to protect her. A romantic adventure like no other!

DESTINY'S WOMAN
(Silhouette Books)

A Native American woman with a wounded heart. A strong, loving
soldier with a sheltering embrace. A love powerful enough to heal...

Available in Feburary!

HER HEALING TOUCH
(Silhouette Special Edition #1519)

A legendary healer. A Special Forces paramedic in need of faith
in love. A passion so strong it could not be denied...

Available in March!

AN HONORABLE WOMAN
(Silhouette Books)

A beautiful pilot with a plan to win back her honor. The man who
stands by her side through and through. The mission that would
take them places no heart should dare go alone...

Where love comes alive™

Visit Silhouette at www.eHarlequin.com   SXSMMDW

eHARLEQUIN.com

For great romance books at great prices,
shop www.eHarlequin.com today!

GREAT BOOKS:
- **Extensive selection** of today's hottest
  books, including **current** releases,
  backlist titles and new **upcoming** books.
- **Favorite authors:** Nora Roberts,
  Debbie Macomber and more!

GREAT DEALS:
- **Save every day:** enjoy great savings
  and special online promotions.
- *Exclusive* **online offers:** FREE books,
  bargain outlet savings, special deals.

EASY SHOPPING:
- Easy, secure, **24-hour shopping** from the
  comfort of your own home.
- **Excerpts, reader recommendations**
  and our **Romance Legend** will help
  you choose!
- **Convenient shipping and
  payment methods.**

**Shop online
at www.eHarlequin.com today!**

INTBB2

If you enjoyed what you just read,
then we've got an offer you can't resist!

Take 2 bestselling
love stories FREE!
Plus get a FREE surprise gift!

Clip this page and mail it to Silhouette Reader Service™

IN U.S.A.	IN CANADA
3010 Walden Ave.	P.O. Box 609
P.O. Box 1867	Fort Erie, Ontario
Buffalo, N.Y. 14240-1867	L2A 5X3

YES! Please send me 2 free Silhouette Special Edition® novels and my free surprise gift. After receiving them, if I don't wish to receive anymore, I can return the shipping statement marked cancel. If I don't cancel, I will receive 6 brand-new novels every month, before they're available in stores! In the U.S.A., bill me at the bargain price of $3.99 plus 25¢ shipping and handling per book and applicable sales tax, if any*. In Canada, bill me at the bargain price of $4.74 plus 25¢ shipping and handling per book and applicable taxes**. That's the complete price and a savings of at least 10% off the cover prices—what a great deal! I understand that accepting the 2 free books and gift places me under no obligation ever to buy any books. I can always return a shipment and cancel at any time. Even if I never buy another book from Silhouette, the 2 free books and gift are mine to keep forever.

235 SDN DNUR
335 SDN DNUS

Name	(PLEASE PRINT)	
Address	Apt.#	
City	State/Prov.	Zip/Postal Code

* Terms and prices subject to change without notice. Sales tax applicable in N.Y.
** Canadian residents will be charged applicable provincial taxes and GST.
  All orders subject to approval. Offer limited to one per household and not valid to current Silhouette Special Edition® subscribers.
® are registered trademarks of Harlequin Books S.A., used under license.

SPED02   ©1998 Harlequin Enterprises Limited

Coming in March 2003, from

Silhouette® Desire®

and _USA TODAY_ bestselling author

SHARON SALA

Amber by Night

**She followed all the rules—
from nine to five!**

From sunup to sundown she
was Amelia Beauchamp, small-
town librarian. But after hours
she was known as miniskirt-
clad cocktail waitress
Amber Champion. And she'd
caught the eye of the town's
biggest rake, Tyler Savage.
This was one savage who
would never be interested in
mousy Amelia. She had to
keep playing the game. For
the stakes were high—love!

*Available in March
at your favorite retail outlet.*

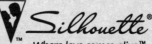

Silhouette®
Where love comes alive™

Visit Silhouette at www.eHarlequin.com   SDABN

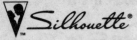

COMING NEXT MONTH

#1525 THE FAMILY PLAN—Gina Wilkins
The McClouds of Mississippi
Attorney Caitlin Briley had spent her life dreaming of career success. But growing feelings for Nathan McCloud, her partner in a small-town law firm, were threatening to change her priorities. Could Nathan convince Caitlin of the importance of family?

#1526 LOVING LEAH—Nikki Benjamin
Years ago, Leah Hayes had been crushed when John Bennett chose her beautiful stepsister over her. Now John was widowed, grieving and struggling to raise his fragile little girl all alone. A still-smitten Leah stepped in as little Gracie's nanny until John got back on his feet. But could she penetrate the wall around the taciturn single dad's heart?

#1527 CALL OF THE WEST—Myrna Temte
Hearts of Wyoming
Jake McBride had always dreamed of owning the Double Circle Ranch and was livid when he learned it had been sold to romance writer Hope DuMaine. Beautiful Hope didn't have the first clue how to run a ranch, so she enlisted Jake's help. As passions rose between the two, it seemed that they may have gotten more than they bargained for....

#1528 A BILLIONAIRE AND A BABY—Marie Ferrarella
The Mom Squad
Sherry Campbell was an ambitious anchorwoman whose career came crashing down around her once she discovered she was pregnant. Determined to make it back to the top of her profession, she landed an interview with reclusive corporate raider St. John (Sin-Jin) Broderick. Could Sin-Jin save her, in more ways than one?

#1529 PLAYING BY THE RULES—Beverly Bird
Readers' Ring
Single mom Amanda Hillman and Sam Case had been the best of friends for years. When they decided they were finished with the singles scene, Amanda and Sam worked out an arrangement to benefit them both—the most important rule being no long-term commitment. Could Sam and Amanda play by the rules and ignore their feelings for each other?

#1530 REFORMING COLE—Ann Roth
Readers' Ring
Zoey Dare had her work cut out for her. As the instructor for a class teaching men how to understand women, headstrong Cole Tyler was just the kind of difficult student she was worried about. But despite their differences, neither of them had any control over the sparks that flew whenever they were together....

SSECNM0203